To Diane
a fellow author!
Rosaleen
R. Myers

HERSELF

Agnes in America

An Epistolary Novel

Rosaleen Rooney Myers

ISBN: 1544026420
ISBN 13: 9781544026428

AUTHOR'S NOTE

My Irish heritage is routed in New York City and Newport, RI. My father's love for the city where he was born in 1905 was palpable. As we walked the streets hand in hand, he'd share stories of his youth and reveal mysteries hidden beyond the facades of the brownstones, the subways, inns and taverns.

There was a time in his youth when his family lived above Pete's Tavern. He showed me the red-roped booth where O'Henry wrote "The Gift of the Magi, and Gramercy Park, open only to residents.

Mom was born in Newport, RI in 1907 and arrived in New York to study nursing at University Hospital. The "lads" from the East Side liked the nurses, and so they met.

In the summer at my Nana's home in Newport, I'd walk the cliffs, swim and bike and visit the estates with my aunts and uncles who had connections through their employment. I played in the great marble hall at the Beechwood Estate, wandered through gardens of impeccable beauty and quietly watched as chefs prepared gala feasts.

Agnes slipped into my head like a soft Irish breeze and blossomed like the Rose of Sharon tree as her story unfolded. Here then is *Herself,* a young Irish immigrant who comes to America in 1905 an traverses these two worlds, using her gifts of brains, beauty, wit and courage to enhance her life.

ACKNOWLEDGEMENTS

Many thanks to my writing colleagues Gayle Aanensen and Rosemary Calabretta for their insights, superb editing and story consultation, and to the Jersey Shore Writers for their encouragement.

NEW YORK CITY – 1905

Mrs. Patrick Logan
Ros Leana Farm
Ballygar, County Galway
Ireland

June 5, 1905

My dear Mum,

It would indeed be a lie if I tell you the journey was a pleasant one, though I thank the Lord above for the second-class ticket that cousin Norah sent from Newport. On days, the seas were rough, but the galley was infused with music and laughter, and if my stomach was well I did an occasional jig.

As we neared our destination the lower decks were opened and this ragtag bunch of Irish pinched together taking deep breaths of salty American air. It is indeed a heart stopping moment to enter New York harbor and set tired eyes on the Lady Liberty, her crown and torch shooting prisms of light, her promise one's faith must believe. My eyes and heart filled with tears at the sight of her and a hushed silence surrounded the usual boisterous lads and ladies. And beyond her, like a curtain rising to the heavens I saw the great New York City. Buildings of uncountable stories rose to the sky, and it seemed from a distance they were almost touching each other, close and proud, saluting and daring this band of newcomers.

The ship docked at a port in the city to allow the first-class passengers to disembark. What a wondrous site it was to see the fancy carriages and footmen usher the passengers in their finery to their waiting cabs. The dock was bustling with masses of workers unloading crates and trunks, and seamen anchoring the ship to port. I've never seen anything like it, even in Dublin, which is indeed a major city of the world.

We then sailed to Ellis Island. Again, I was awestruck by the massive edifice that came into view, its four pinnacles rising like a cathedral. I was terrified, I must confess. The authorities herded us in a line down the gangplank and into a place I've never seen the likes of before, nor ever will again. It was surely one hundred feet high, and a corn field in width, with curved half-moon windows high near the ceiling. I thought there may be birds nesting there.

Hundreds of benches filled the floor and we were led there to sit and wait for our names to be called. I must say that these Americans and quite efficient. They took my papers and entered my name, Agnes Bridget Logan. It is a simple name, I think, but it has been said that foreign names have been changed in the interest of simplicity.

A doctor checked me quickly and determined I was a healthy specimen of Irish womanhood, praise be to God. There are those who are sent back, I have heard, but we all made it through, our lovely Irish boat full. We were ushered out with our meager belongings to a ferry that took us across the bay.

We pulled into a place called South Ferry and I now put my immigrant feet on true American soil. As you know, it had been arranged for me to stay at Maureen Galvin's inn until I could get settled and continue my journey to Newport. I was assured someone would be there to cart me away, but it is almost impossible to describe the noise and confusion of that moment. I thought I might wind up a rag picker on the streets.

Horses and carts and vendors selling chestnuts and hot cider and coal and vegetables and whiskey all yelled for attention. The pier was filled with people calling out names and raising signs on sticks, jostling each other to find their prey. I held my carpetbag tight, adjusted my shawl and pushed into the crowd. I thought if I could make this journey I will indeed end up where I am supposed to be. And then above the crowd I saw the sign with my name scrawled on it, and heard someone calling "Agnes Logan, Agnes Logan, Agnes Logan." I blessed myself and did a little genuflection in gratitude, bumped into a whiskey cart and found the caller. He was a big specimen of a man, with a ruddy complexion and a red beard. Feeling like a tiny bird, I put down my bag, touched his strong arm and said, "I am Agnes Logan."

"And a fine prize you are," he said. "John Galvin here. Maureen will be having some hot tea for ya. Now, stay close and follow me."

He took my bag, elbowed his way through the throng, carving a path for us. The sounds of the rowdy crowd faded and we hurried along. My feet, in their worn old brown brogans had a time keeping pace with his long strides, but I held on to my tam and forged on. We turned a corner and I found us on a crooked little street nestled like a nugget in the clamor of this place. A wooden signpost with an old mare tied up to it read "Maiden Lane." The buildings were only about five stories high with shops of all kinds of things. There was a haberdasher, and a butcher, and a greengrocer. A fish monger was selling his catch. The metal fire escapes held lines of clothes drying in the breeze and the faces of little children peeked from the alleys.

Nestled between the alleys and the shops was a door painted bright kelly green, a good omen I would say. Above it a bright white and green sign pronounced, "Galvin's Emerald Inn," and beneath that, "no transients." I guess one has to be Irish and off the boat to be welcome here. The door opened and lovely round woman with eyes the color of the sea and chestnut hair tied in a bun reached out and took me in a hug, exclaiming.

"Agnes Logan! At long last. You darlin' girl, you surely are exhausted from the arduous journey. But, let me look at you. Oh, saints alive. Your mum said you were a raven beauty with your black hair and dark eyes and surely she was right."

When I caught my breath, still a bit overwhelmed by this embrace, I whispered, "Maureen, Maureen Galvin?"

"One and the same, now come. John will take your bag upstairs. I've a sweet room for you facing the yard in the back. Can you fancy that? I've a tiny yard, enough to grow some potatoes and beans and a stray tomato when the sun comes on it."

Mum, I was tired to the bone, and a sweet room seemed heaven had found me.

Your loving daughter,
Agnes

Miss Agnes Logan
c/o Galvin's Emerald Inn
10 Maiden Lane
New York, New York
USA

May 30, 1905

My darlin' Agnes,

It was with a sad but hopeful heart I bid you farewell a fortnight ago. Your sweet face smiling at me as you bordered Georgie Rooney's bus to the boat is forever etched in my heart. But you have always been our brightest and most fearless child, stronger than your brothers in the ways of the world, I believe.

As you well know, Mike and Patrick like Pa are simple Irish farmers, working the soil, gathering the peat and tending the animals.

Pa would be worn to the bone without their good nature, ceaseless work and pint at the end of the day. I still light a candle now and then for a spouse for one or both of them even though they are needed here, but my senses whisper they may be confirmed bachelors, blushing at the site of a pretty lass.

Charlie is showing his independence. He finished his terms and Father Shea had him in hand, keeping his cowlick in place so to speak. We always pray for a priest, but Charlie is not the one, so unless I am blessed like St. Ann and bear another we will be priestless. He has heard about this company in Belfast, that British stronghold, that builds seafaring ships for companies all over the world. It is so big and they need many workers. They have an apprentice program at the Belfast College of Technology to learn a proper trade. It is the dawn of a new century, Agnes, with many wonders in the world. He's been writing letters. We will see.

Maggie Flynn was over for tea. Well, Fey is bethroed to James O'Connell, but then you must have known something was in the wind, being so close to her and all. I saw you girls sauntering past the apothecary more than once, and she did have her shining red head set on him. They are all agog she has landed such a prosperous one. He seems a fine lad, though a bit pinched around the lips.

Norah has assured me that Maureen and John will take fine care of you whilst in New York. I do not know the Galvin's, but word has it that Norah married well when she settled in Newport. She being twelve years older than you it may be so that you don't remember her as a child. She crossed ten years ago, when still a lass like yourself. I await your missive of the journey and the sites of the city.

Your loving Mum
Rose

Mrs. Patrick Logan
Ros Leana Farm
Ballygar, County Galway
Ireland

June 7, 1905

Dear Mum,

I was so exhausted I slept like a rock that had fallen to the bottom of the sea. When I awoke, I lay quietly for a moment with my eyes closed. I didn't hear the splash of the waves rocking the boat on my journey, or the sounds of the bird's morning song and soft Irish breeze like home. I heard a loud whistle, a tug boat or a siren, the wheels of carts on the cobblestone streets, children calling to each other, doors slamming, steps on the stairs. The smell of Irish bacon and warm scones urged me out of my confusion and lethargy and I opened my eyes and glanced around the room I had not noticed the night before.

T'was a small room but exceedingly charming. I lay upon a brass bed covered with a colorful quilt of bright reds and blues, and white shutters were open letting in the morning breeze. The room was white and dark wooden beams crossed the ceiling. My duffel bag sat upon a bench next to an intricately carved mahogany armoire. I thought this surely was far too grand for my meager things. Next to the bed a small table with a lace runner held a white china basin and pitcher of water. I slipped out of bed and went to the window. Sure enough there was a garden below me, as neatly planted as any at home, but far smaller, of course. The leaves of a lovely tree whispered to me.

I freshened up and followed the scents to the kitchen. Maureen sat at a long table, writing in a journal. "Just doin' the books," she said, "How was your sleep? Come, have breakfast." Good Lord, the saints had come to save me, I thought, as I filled my aching self with such wonderful food. "Eat, girl. You've been living on roots and bread for too long."

I tidied up my place and brought the dishes over to the sink. To my astonishment there was running water! Maureen stood against the counter, her blue eyes twinkling at my bemusement. She said they were blessed not to live in a tenement, crowded like rats with smells and disease like so many of the poor immigrants who come to these shores.

Well, Mum, I knew that the Galvin's had some money tucked away from God knows where - given the plight of Ireland, but my new surroundings were full of wonders, some of which I had yet to encounter.

I knew that I must leave to make me way to Newport to find work in one of the mansions there, but my secret wish was that I might partake in some of the city's wonders before I said goodbye. As I was pondering my situation, John arrived, his bulk filling the doorway. "How's our girl today?" he asked. I said I was fine but a bit bamboozled by all I had seen and heard in these short twenty-four hours. He laughed heartily and said my adventure was just beginning.

"Here's the thing, Aggie, me girl," he said. "We live in a great city, bursting with energy and hard living. Time for a cuppa in a moment of quiet. But you've had a hard journey and are part of the family so I've arranged a bit of treat while you'll be stayin' here."

I was busting to discover what he meant, but I knew I must be on my way soon. I began to speak of when I should be leaving.

"The steamship runs every three days, leavin' tomorrow, but that's way too soon, since we're just now enjoyin' your company. We're thinkin' you'll be stayin' a week, then you'll be makin' your way to Newport. It's not a terrible journey like the one you just made. It leaves in the evening and you awake to the cliffs of Newport in the morning."

A week! A week in New York! I could barely catch my breath.

"Now, Aggie, we here are all workin' hard to keep this place in profitable means, and I have my taxi business so to speak, and work on the docks when extra strong arms are needed. There's a young fella belongs to Mrs. O'Connor at the bakers. He's just a youngster, but he's very industrious and knows his way around the city. He'll be your guide. He's a bit of a charmer and rides the electric cars for free sometimes, but don't be followin' his lead, you'll wind up in the poky."

Electric cars? What is he talking about? I never heard of such a thing. Just as I'm about to show my ignorance one more time, the doorbell clangs.

"He be here," says John.

He's a skinny long drink of water, not completely filled out, about fourteen years I would venture to guess. He had a head of curly black hair and a cap jauntily pushed toward the back, as if gravity didn't exist. His knickers and his shirt were nicely pressed.

"Pleased to meet ya, Chipper O'Connor at your service," he said and extended his hand.

"Now run up and gather your things," said Maureen, "and be on your way with Chipper. And, Chipper, don't be movin' too fast in these streets, Aggie doesn't know her way around here. Stay close and be careful."

"Ain't I always?" he said with a wink.

"Oh, you got the divil in you, young man, behave."

"Yes, ma'am."

I grabbed my shawl, tightened the laces on my brogans, and with a smile of trepidation and expectation, off I went with Chipper into the bustling street.

Oh, mum, my eyes are tired and I have a letter from Norah here. I promise I'll tell you of my adventures soon. Keep well,

Your loving daughter,
Agnes

Miss Agnes Logan
c/o Galvin's Emerald Inn
10 Maiden Lane
New York, New York

June 7, 1905

Dear Agnes,

Don't let anyone call you Aggie. My good name, praises be, cannot be shortened. Since we heard of no disaster at sea, we wish you welcome to this new land of ours. The post is sometimes slow, but we find luck with the steamship from here to New York if we plan properly with the mail carrier. My hope is this will reach you on your arrival.

Sure, John and Maureen are grand people, he being my husband Tom's brother and all. Unlike Tommy, who craves the salt air and greenery, John hitched his wagon to that boisterous city the likes of which I could not wait to leave. He said the energy and promise of prosperity kept his size eleven feet planted in the rock. I've heard it is built on a rock, must surely be a large one.

He and Maureen, from the Wilans of Killarney, met at an Irish social on Fulton Street and hear them tell it was love at first sight. Imagine. I'm told there is a fish market there of great proportions and hordes of people vying for a best price. Perhaps you may see it. No doubt it is quite odorous.

It can only be a distress for you to have your destiny in the arms of others, no matter how loving. My heart feels the tears you must have shed leaving your mum, Rose, but we will embrace you if that can soothe your sadness.

In my correspondence with your Mum it seemed you would flourish in this sparkling spot of beauty we now call home. I told her of the cliffs and the flowers and the elegant estates that border Bellevue Avenue. Your courage and trust are an example of the brave Irish spirit born of both survival and adventure.

We have a green and white house on a narrow little street that weaves its way to the ocean. A fine porch allows for baskets of herbs and plants and flowers which leave an aura of the scent of Ireland. Tommy has a sweet vegetable garden for our needs. His shop of hardware and tools on Thames Street has filled a need much to our delight, and his carpentry skills are in demand.

There is much work to be had here for young ladies such as yourself in the clean and safe estates of the filthy rich. When I think of the fine learning we had and the gift of all the reading and writing so diligently taught it does not warm me for you to go into service. I do know from Mary Lynch, nee Logan, from Uncle Pat's branch of the family, that there are many servants in these mansions who perform special chores. Why I've heard there is one in the Breakers who just arranges flowers and a butler for the butler's pantry. Imagine that. Mary is a fine cook and in demand can you believe for special parties. They call her a pastry chef. Imagine.

These fancy people call their estates "summer cottages" can you believe, as if the wealthy were like the rest of poor humanity in this world. Oh, I must not taint your sweet young soul, so forgive my Irish ire.

Come soon. You will be welcomed and loved and we will add another Irish Rose to our vine.

Your cousin,
Norah

Mrs. Patrick Logan
Ros Leana
Ballygar, County Galway
Ireland

June 9, 1905

Dear Mum,

In my hand, I have a lovely note from cousin Norah, so kind and generous. I also have your letter which must have crossed with mine. 'Tis true Fey set her burnished head for James O'Connell. I would not presume to question her choice, and perhaps she will bring some levity to his rather stern visage. The ways of love have not yet found me so I am but a novice in the mysteries of the heart. Perhaps as I venture forth in this new world I will find a purpose other than service. Here in this city women are teachers and nurses and something called an amanuensis. You, who have always been so wise, said it be the dawn of a new century, and I feel my bones on the cusp of a great adventure. Surely young Charlie and I seem to share the spirit of adventure and if he is to move further into the world he will do well with his quick wit and fine brain, although it will be a strain on you and Pa to have both of us gone from the nest.

Three days hence I shall set sail for Newport and I am told it is a pleasant trip, unlike the fierce journey across the cold Atlantic. Newport sounds like a bit of Ireland as she describes the rocky cliffs and green lawns to the sea.

As you know, I am to find employment there if that is my destiny. I will confess to you, but not to worry, I have seen such wonders here in the New York City it will be a trial to not enthuse to others about these feelings.

Maureen sent me off with a young lad, Chipper O'Connor, to see some of the city.

He whisked me down Maiden Lane, tipping his hat to the ladies scrubbing the stoops and hanging their laundry. We passed the fish monger and smithy. I had to watch my feet for fear of the droppings. But, in but a quick turn here and turn there we were on the great Broadway. It is surely an apt name for I never in my life have seen such a grand wide street. Ladies in fine attire and gentlemen all in black were bustling all around. The people here are very quick and one needs care not to get knocked down by the hoard. I say that with glee for the energy here sets my heart racing, just to see faces from so many places about on their business and pleasure.

Carriages and horses were everywhere, swerving and halting to avoid the magical electric trolleys. Oh, Mum, what a thing to see, a long car open in front and back, with straw seats filled with all these bustling and busy people. Chipper grabbed hold of my arm tightly and said to keep close to him. So, I did and we walked along. We passed elegant shops with fine clothes and goods, even watches and pendants of gold and platinum. Eating establishments with gilded mirrors and crystal glasses and staff in starched black and white seemed busy with people of importance, I am sure.

I asked Chipper if we could go for a ride on the trolley. It cost 2 cents a ride. He took off his cap and bowed to me like a fancy gentleman and said, "Follow me, madam." I laughed heartily at his bravado and did just that.

The dust of the road swirled around us as he hailed the trolley. The conductor smiled and said, "Chipper O'Connor, are ye lookin' for a freebie again?"

"Just a wee discount," he said, "I be here with my friend straight from County Galway." The conductor gave me once over look and said, "A fine lass to light our city, then, one cent."

I hitched up my skirt to climb the iron steps, the trolley clanged a loud bell, and before I could even sit we began to move along at a speed I've never encountered before, so I scrambled quickly to a seat. Chipper stood up and gave his seat to an elegant lady dressed in blue with a feathered scarf tickling her face. He bent over me and whispered, "Ostrich feathers." Well, I have never seen such regalia, and felt shabby in my simple black cotton shirtwaist. I needn't have given myself a second look for soon the trolley was filled with such a host of the most unusual persons. Well, Mum, I saw a Chinaman, I did, with a long black braid down his back and a coat of many colors. He was carrying a crate filled with chickens and he scurried to the back of the trolley. Chipper seemed to know a lot of the people, even two Italian gentlemen who greeted him, "Cheeper, Cheeper, bon journo," they said. Just when my breath was about to leave me with excitement, he said, "Look, Agnes, to your right, that's City Hall."

This is surely one of the important cities of the world by the size of their City Hall, like a castle with white marble colonnades and a great green park. Chipper looked into his little black book that seems to hold his secrets and pronounced it was French Renaissance style. The trolley waited there for a moment and some very important looking gentlemen boarded. They tipped their hats and smiled at everyone, and chipper whispered, "Councilmen."

And so, in but a wink, I had seen an ostrich feather, a Chinaman, greeted two Italians and smiled at councilmen of this amazing city, but had but gone a short mile if even that. Oh, yes, we continued on, passing the horses and carriages as the trolley clanged and my heart grew wild with excitement. I fret so to leave you at such a juncture of my tale, but the day has waned and my thoughts are scattered as my mind swirls with images of this new and amazing world.

Your loving daughter,
Agnes

Mrs. Thomas Galvin
41 Dixon Street
Newport, Rhode Island

June 10, 1905

Dear Cousin Norah,

Maureen was hustling over to the ship to post a letter to you so I took the opportunity to pen a quick note. Your delightful missive was awaiting me on my arrival. It was an arduous journey as you are acquainted with but my chill and fatigue were vanquished by the tender ministrations of Maureen and John. I do not doubt that you would find their charming inn a comfort as well, if you ever venture back this way. I do gather from your note that you do not find this city one of comfort, although I have been having a "boisterous" time seeing the sites in the company of one young Chipper O'Connor, a fine guide and friend of the Galvin's.

After a wicked day of riding the electric trolley all the way to Herald Square, and a breathless walk to the magnificent Madison Square Garden with its turret of thirty-four stories I was beyond exhilaration. Today Maureen and Chipper walked us over to that odorous Fulton Fish Market filled with hundreds of vendors and a thousand, if not more, people all clamoring and bargaining. Maureen purchased some lovely salmon, laughing that these creatures do not leap up like they do in Ireland unto your plate. My eyes then caught a most magnificent bridge that seemed to be defying gravity. Chipper gallantly offered to walk me there and over it we went, and I could feel the slight sway as we reached the center and I looked to the New York Bay heading out to the Atlantic. It is called the Brooklyn Bridge, of all things, and I would think that it should have a more regal name, like the Bridge to Heaven, or something such. Chipper, always the talker, took out his little black notebook and informed me it was indeed the longest suspension bridge in the world. Now, never having heard of such a thing, I was flummoxed but felt the grandness of its magnificence.

Oh, Norah, I will be in Newport soon, and on to more dutiful things, I am sure, but this journey has been one of wonder, and my heart is full. With fondness, I look forward to seeing you and my Irish cousins anon.

Your cousin,
Agnes

Mr. an Mrs. Thomas Galvin
41 Dixon Street
Newport, Rhode Island

June 10, 1905

Dear Norah and Tom,

I rushed over to the steamship company to post this with hope that it would arrive before Agnes makes her journey. She is a beautiful and adventurous young lady with a bit of the sass to her, not that she was anything but charming and grateful to us. I have to say when our young friend, Chipper O'Conner took her in hand for the tour of the city she came back flushed with excitement, no fear in her slim frame.

When she learned that young ladies worked in real positions here as nurses, and teachers, and in business, she could not contain her eagerness to explore this reality, a reality I suppose that this melting pot of humanity offers, unlike more provincial places. It rather amazed me how easily she stepped into these dusty city streets with such glee.

Tomorrow evening, we will hitch up the buggy and ride her over to the steamship in the East River for her overnight voyage to Newport. I trust that Thomas or one of the family will be there to greet her, as planned. Of course, I have fond and lovely memories of your sparkling city where we spent our honeymoon. I was fortunate to have a peek inside The Breakers thanks to Raymond Burns, who tends the gardens beautifully. It is so lovely of you to take Agnes in hand, and I trust that you and Thomas's connections will settle her in a fine estate.

With fondness and love,

Your sister-in-law,
Maureen

Miss Fey Flynn
Bracken Lane
Ballygar, County Galway
Ireland

June 11, 1905

My dearest friend Fey,

It is with wondrous joy at your wit and charm that I congratulate you on snaring your heartthrob James. Oh, how we plotted, under the Rose of Sharon tree, to "accidentally" meet him in our sweet little village of Ballygar. I think we scared him half to death, he with his stern visage and proper ways, but I have to say he certainly has a handsome look with his dark Irish eyes and tall frame. There was nothing to do but keep a straight face and hide my glee the day you "tripped" in the mud and fell straight into his arms. He was so flustered when you looked up at him with your big green eyes I doubt he'll ever recover, which portends well for a long happy life together.

As you know from pouring over my "itinerary", a lovely word doesn't you think, I have been with Maureen and John Galvin for the past three days and am leaving for Newport soon on a steamship, "The Puritan." I have found this amazing city, however, to match the beat of my heart and it is with sadness I leave it. I am told that Newport is much like Ireland in its natural state of beauty, and that should ease my sadness. Perhaps there is a Rose of Sharon I can linger by and think of you, my dear, sweet friend, embarking on her own journey. Here I am, but a young soul, bidding farewell twice in such a short time to people and places. It wears on my heart and burdens me, but I am of adventurous spirit and shall welcome the challenges that await me for now.

Mum should be receiving several long letters detailing my adventures here. Do drop by to see her and perhaps share a cup of tea and think of me. With all my love to you and your James,

With love,
Agnes

NEWPORT, RI 1905

In Service

Mrs. Patrick Logan
Ros Leana Farm
Ballygar, County Galway
Ireland

June 15, 1905

Dearest Mum,

I pray I find you fit and strong and in your usual high spirits. Despite the toil of the farm I trust you find time for a spot of tea near a cozy fire. It has been barely a week since I disembarked at South Ferry and the whirlwind of my travels has left me breathless.

I have arrived, again. The eight- hour overnight trip from New York to Newport on the elegant steamship was a heady experience. Although I had a small bunk, my night was spent in the glittering salons watching the dancing and listening to the music. It is indeed a very democratic ship, unlike the one that carried me here, for everyone is invited to partake in the joviality. Well, Mrs. Astor was on board and I met her lady's maid, Eileen Burns. She had not much time for me as she was tending to her lady, but we formed a quick bond. If the spirits of the saints so desire I may be fortunate to find such a position which is considered of high rank. I do not think I would do well as a scullery maid, not that I demean them in any way, but I do have a bit of my nose in the air.

Newport was indeed a lovely sight from the sea. Its cliffs and green lawns sweep to the rocks, and the haze of the morning did remind me of home. My heart was anxious with anticipation to explore the byways, but I knew I must calm my impetuous nature for a bit. It has been over a dozen years since I've seen Norah and she was my age when she left, so I was fearful I may not find her, and heavens knows she would not recognize the eight-year-old annoying cousin as the young lady I am today. But, there she was with a handsome man beside her, waving a sign. We embraced happily and Thomas laughed and said it was sure that we were both from the same branch with our dark eyes and hair. The two boys, Thomas Jr. and Fitz were beside themselves with excitement at this new cousin. Norah fussed with me and cried a bit, then Thomas pulled up an elegant carriage and we headed down a narrow but very bustling cobblestone street called Thames Street.

When we arrived, the neighbors were about, curious no doubt, as to the newcomer. Norah brought me up to a wee attic room with a small brass bed and white painted bureau. Just think, twice in one week I have my own little room. There is a window near a willow tree and the scent of honeysuckle wafts on the breeze. The aroma of honeysuckle is everywhere, sprung up like ocean perfume in the mist.

Oh, Mum, there is so much to absorb, and I believe the clock in my heart is still ticking New York, New York. I pray to St. Mary for fortitude and acceptance, for tomorrow I am to have an interview at the grandest of estates, The Breakers. Love to Pa and the boys and light a candle if you will for my destiny.

Your loving daughter,
Agnes

Mr. and Mrs. John Galvin
Galvin's Emerald Inn
10 Maiden Lane
New York, New York

June 17, 1905

Dear Maureen and John,

She has arrived and does have a bit of flash about her. Our usual quiet little Dixon Street was all abuzz with curiosity as our carriage pulled up. George Shea, whose main occupation is sitting on the porch with a pint, made a pretense of trimming the hedges. His rather rheumy eyes shot open like firecrackers at the first look at her. Ray Burns was all burnished up with an armful of flowers from his garden, and Mary Lynch dropped off a lemon meringue pie. Despite all the attention she seemed most composed, gracious and proper. That is a relief.

I quickly got her settled in the dormer room, much to her delight. It is very simple, but adequate. It was her wish to walk to the sea, up High Dixon and across to the cliffs. Fortunately, young Sonny Lynch was out doing some chores for his mother, Mary, and leapt at the chance to escort this beautiful rare bird. Being he's only fifteen I was not alarmed. He took her in hand for a bit of a walk along to the Forty Steps to see the ocean.

I have set an appointment with the housekeeper at The Breakers, Mrs. Holmes. Tom is acquainted with her through his business with the estate. I hear she runs an impeccable staff. Our girl will have to be on her best behavior if she is to pass muster with the likes of Mrs. Holmes. She is, as is the fashion, a British import. I will see that Agnes has her shoes polished and her wild bundle of hair tied in a neat knot. All the estates are in a frenzy of preparation for the American Royalty to arrive within the week. Even the sidewalks of Bellevue Avenue have been swept and scrubbed and the lampposts shined to glimmer. Oh, what a fuss for those entitled, but it is income for the less fortunate.

My thoughts and prayers are with you as always in that tumultuous place you call home.

Your sister-in-law,
Norah

Mrs. Patrick Logan
Ros Leana Farm
Ballygar, County Galway
Ireland

June 20, 1905

Dear Mum,

I be here in Norah's sweet and tidy home, but I fear not for long. It was no sooner then I breathed a sigh and closed my eyes to the sounds of the foghorn, that I was to learn I would be off to The Breakers for a meeting with the housekeeper. Norah is an efficient one. No doubt she could run one of these estates without much of a blink. She is not taken with these rich dandies and told me to hold my head high, but to keep a humble demeanor. 'Tis a quandary.

I set off with Raymond in the morning, his wagon filled with sod and seeds and tools for the garden. We passed a manse on the corner, Bellecourt, then along Bellevue Avenue to a wide shaded street called Ochre Point. He pulled up to very imposing high gates with sculptures atop them and a workman came forward, tipped his head to Raymond, and opened them. As we drove down the long driveway the immense estate came into view and I thought surely I would be but a tiny speck in such splendor. Raymond told me it was one acre in size and built of limestone with marble appointments and a slate roof and that the ten-foot carved teak entry doors are balanced so perfectly one can open them with a finger. In but a short ride I traveled from a simple narrow street with clapboard houses to a world beyond my humble experience.

When we approached the servants entrance, Raymond said Mrs. Holmes was held in high esteem for her position at The Breakers and she was one to be envied. I do not quite understand the envy of service, but I fear I will learn.

A kitchen maid said to wait. Servants were scrubbing and polishing preparing for the arrival of the Vanderbilt's, who I have heard are the richest people in America. The little maid led me to Mrs. Holmes who has her own office down a corridor. She was a tall woman, dressed in black, but had that rather pasty faced complexion of the English. She motioned for me to enter, but did not ask me to sit. "Agnes Logan, is that correct?" she asked. I said, "Yes, ma'am," in my most humble voice. Now, I knew Tom had kindly asked her to see me, and she spoke of her high praise of him, and that maybe I would do. She told me to show her my hands and turn in a circle and walked around me. "I understand you have never been in service?" she asked. I answered, "No, ma'am," then I said,

"Yes, ma'am," and I think I flushed a bit. She looked me up and down with eyes like the flint of the fire and announced I was a fine specimen. Can you imagine Mum, a specimen? I bristled at that and held me head higher.

She handed me a book and said to start reading aloud. I did keeping in mind the oratory skills learned at St. Michaels. She said I seemed to have some breeding and since I was literate, I would do after I was polished up and trained. Polished up! I never. Not a smile crossed her face. She said I would be trained as a lady's maid for the guests of Mrs. Vanderbilt and to come the next day with my bags packed as she had no more time for me.

I backed out very servant like and gulped the air of the garden and the sea as the tears came. They were due, my dear Mum. They were due. Now I am worn and will bid you a soft goodnight.

Your loving daughter,
Agnes

Miss Agnes Logan
41 Dixon Street
Newport, Rhode Island

June 25, 1905

Dear Agnes,

I post this in care of your cousin Norah on Dixon Street in hopes she will pass it to you. Since our lively journey on the steamship to Newport, I have settled in with Mrs. Astor for another summer at her mansion, Beechwood. It is there you can find me. My thoughts have been with you, hoping that you have found employment and are comfortable in your shoes. This is my third summer here and I am in my place now, but my thoughts hearken back to my early days in this new country and I think of you.

There is a loneliness in service even though beauty surrounds one. A spare moment to visit and share would be lovely for us both. Let us try to meet.

With kind thoughts,
Eileen Burns

Mrs. Patrick Logan
Ros Leana Farm
Ballygar, County Galway
Ireland

July 3, 1905

Dear Mum,

The days have been a rush of learning and work. Me, a lady's maid, of all things, to the rich guests who need a hand pulling up their drawers. Mrs. Holmes took me in hand when I arrived with me dusty carpetbag. I wear a plain black dress with a white collar and when needed an apron.

She is a bit of a Brit, that one, but swished me quickly through the great marble hall, up the velvet covered staircase to the fancy suites and bedrooms, then up another flight to the servants' quarters. If I run up and down like this every day my figure will stay trim. It seems I'm always telling you about my room, but I do have a fine one in the estate here with an iron bedstead, a rocking chair, and fine dresser and mirror. Mrs. Vanderbilt, I've been told, believes in fine accommodations for her staff. Of course, the bell to summon me is ever present. So many bells for so many servants. Times, it sounds like a rusty church bell ringing day and night.

When the lady herself arrived her lady's maid, Ingrid, a Swedish girl, took me in hand with a bit of her nose in the air, and flounced off with me trailing behind. Mrs. Vanderbilt smiled wanly and gestured to the corner where I remained to observe the morning ritual. Oh, what a fuss of silk and linen and pearls. Ingrid even put her bloody shoes on. I must temper myself for these chores. Ingrid told me that Countess Murzurski was arriving in a week and I must be ready to serve her.

When I finally escaped, I slipped into the kitchen and had tea with cook and the chamber maid, Ginnie, who soothed my nerves. Then, a gift came to me, like an angel on my shoulder. Norah came with a letter from Eileen Burns, Ms. Astor's lady's maid, who I met on my journey. I penned a quick note to her and we managed to meet when our duties allowed. To see her again was a blessing for she has been in such a place as me. We sat on the cliffs between our two mansions looking towards home and a life where such pleasures of the rich is a distant as the mist that forms from the sea. She gently explained her daily chores, and reminded me that we were to be seen but not heard. So, I be dumb, for now.

Praise to Eileen and not uppity Ingrid, for when the Countess arrived I performed well, though the saints only know how. The Countess Barbara is an American heiress, a title searcher, I am told. She can have her waxy older husband with his slick mustache. He seems to have a bit of a leer for me. I'm told by Eileen that we maids must often escape the clutches of the so called fine gentlemen with idle hands.

The Countess is a lively one, a thin pretty young lady with a bit of a sparkle in her eye. I unpacked her trunk and pressed her things, praying I was doing it right. Ingrid haughtily rescued a ball gown that almost burst into flames from the hot iron, and went storming off like I was an eedjit. I hung her things and neatly put her tidies away and waited, holding my breath. I drew her bath and held her robe. She said she was tired from the journey and would have supper in her room. Praise to heaven. I survived my first day as a lady's maid.

She perked up alright and likes to be out and about with lunches and teas and shopping on Bellevue Avenue, where all the swells meet. If there is any fun in this, it be that I go with her to carry her packages, and keep her person tidy. It be said the custom here is to walk behind your mistress as the royalty do in England, but she says this is America and she won't have it. So, we stroll along together, me in my white day dress and she in an elegant linen suit. The other servants think it be odd she escapes the mansion, but it may be she's escaping that slimy Count. In between her visits and luncheons, I have time to breathe and sit in a sun-dappled park, and send a prayer for me freedom from the price of wealth. I'm in my room, but will soon be summoned by her bell for the evening dress up. Give the boys a hearty hug.

Your loving daughter,
Agnes

Miss Agnes Logan
The Breakers
Domestic Mail
Ochre Point Avenue
Newport, Rhode Island
USA

August 1, 1905

Dear Sis,

Mum's been sharin' your letters and I fess up I'm a bit lazy in the writin' department. What with helpin' on the land with the summer crops and animal care, I've had little time specially since I've been crammin' the books with extra studies. I had to send my grades and a note from Father Shea to Belfast, a nerve-wracking thing to say the least, especially without your good hand and brain. I'd ride to the post each day, and spotted Fey cooing around the pharmacy no doubt impatient for her wedding. When the letter came, I ran straight to Father Shea for I would be too ashamed if it was bad news to share with Mum and Pa. I handed it to him to open and held my breath like we used to do to see who could hold it the longest. He told me to stop turnin' blue. They want me Sis. Yes, they do. Here I am now, off to the Belfast School of Technology. They said depending on my "aptitude" I will be placed in a training program to build the new steel ships. I've heard their dockyard is a sight to see with hundreds of men earning a decent wage.

Belfast is indeed another country. 'Tis a day's ride on the railroad, and I change in Dublin for points west. I scraped some coins together by working as a bar boy at night in the Brian Brew though Mum felt it be an occasion of sin. Still, I pay my own way.

Mum says you are in fine form as the lady's maid to the richest people in America. Well, that's a plumb of a start. Send a post home when you have time as the whole bunch are in a dither with my leavin' now its arrived.

Your best brother,
Charlie

Miss Agnes Logan
The Breakers
Domestic Mail
Ochre Point Avenue
Newport, Rhode Island
USA

August 5, 1905

My darlin' Agnes,

Our little one is gone. Georgie Rooney took him to Roscommon to board the train. I wept. Two of you off in the western wind like thistle in the Spring. Pat and Micky are a bit solemn losing their young bro to tease, but the summer was a bountiful one and the days still long and bright. I hold my head high for the paths you and Charlie walk. The biddies in town do get my goat when they "tsk, tsk" about two gone like you were some bloody cows instead of me own flesh and blood. I tell them you have a high station in the grandest estate in the richest place in America and that Charlie will be an engineer, mind you, an engineer! If that be the case.

Pa says that if we need help come spring, there are a few layabouts always looking for a quick coin at the pub and we can spare a bit, praise God. The farm is in fine fettle. Pat painted the shutters of the cottage a lively green and the barn has a new whitewash. We are indeed a picture of farming prosperity, even if it be meager by high hifalutin' standards.

Today I am going to find material to make a dress for Fey's wedding. Days come when she rides over on Blackie for word of you. Her life, too, is about to change marrying that James O'Connell. He is a bit stern though it not be my concern. When I see her ridin' like the wind on that horse of hers with her red hair flying and her cheeks all flushed, a tinge of worry disturbs me. But, no mind, I sound like a busy biddy.

You remain in my prayers, my precious and brave Agnes.

Your loving mum
Rose

Mr. Charles Logan
Belfast College of Technology
Dormitory Three
300 Victoria Blvd.
Belfast, Northern Ireland
United Kingdom

August 15, 1905

Dear Charlie,

Here we both be on a high adventure now. For sure they want you, my fine bright brother. Keep your cowlick down, your eyes straight ahead, and your nose in the books and you'll be grand. 'Tis true I serve the rich and have a decent post with a fine lady, though my dream is to make something better of meself. I keep me head high as Mrs. Holmes, the terrifying British Housekeeper who runs this ship of a mansion like an eagle, over her prey. I am blessed to have a good friend in Eileen Burns, another lovely Irish lass employed by the Astor's. I have fine quarters here, and Norah and Tom and the boys to visit on my day off.

Newport is a crystalline place, with the sea all around and the aromas of home, and I be grateful for the comforts I have. Yet, I yearn to get back to the New York City. Oh, Charlie, to see it would thrill your soul. Now, you too are in a big bustling place, so if you have a day explore and discover the thrill of a city. You are on a path to a good life, so stay strong and smart. Keep your back straight and your head high, when you are not studying that is. Mum was sad when you left, that 'tis true, but she is proud of us and brags about town to the old hags.

You are close to my heart, always.

Your loving sister,
Agnes

Mrs. Patrick Logan
Rose Leana Farm
Ballygar, County Galway
Ireland

August 20, 1905

Dear Mum,

My thoughts are sad this day as the summer wanes and the crickets tell me that soon the fall will arrive. The reach of home widens as each day passes, even here where the air smells of honeysuckle and the dew on the grass is like Ireland in the morning.

Raymond Burns fixed up an old bike for me and Eileen and I went for a cycle around the Ocean Drive. The salt spray and scent of seaweed and grass touched of home as we wound miles along the sea and past the rocky coast. We stopped to rest at a small cove nestled like a precious jewel between the cliffs. We picked our way down to the water's edge where an old rowboat bobbed, as empty and alone as I felt. Mum, if God had transported me back to Galway Bay, I would awaken from this dream and be home, and my legs would cycle me down the road and around the bend to find you. When the tears came to me eyes, Eileen took me hand and we dipped our fingers in the sea, blessed ourselves and sent a prayer to our loved ones.

Soon she will be leaving for New York City with Mrs. Astor, but I do not know my fate yet in the household. Many of the staff make the journey to the mansion on 57th Street in New York City, but the Supervisor of the estate and his wife, Mr. and Mrs. Bauerband, will remain at the Carriage House and maintain help. Oh, Mum, I can taste the excitement of that glorious city, but fear I will left in the dust to only God knows what. Norah says there be many jobs to fill even in the darker days of winter, and I must share her trust.

It be sad when Countess Barbara leaves for she has indeed stayed the summer and we have found a bond, a bit to me surprise and delight. On the night of the Fourth of July, that day of American Independence from our British oppressors, the whole household watched the amazing fireworks over the ocean. I saw her take a hankie to her eye and I reached to touch her hand, a very brazen move for such a servant. But there was a sadness about her I expect she covered with all the gadding about. She held me hand and with tear filled eyes just said, "Oh, Agnes, I will miss my America."

The Count departed a bit ago. No doubt he awaits her presence in his Hungarian castle that by the looks of him it is probably a dark, dank place. I have come to care for her and fear her sparkle will diminish, for I have learned that wealth can be a burden.

Even though Charlie and me are gone, Mum, we go with great love, a gift that not be bought with the riches of the world. He has a chance to make something of hisself in this world of new wonders. I, too, wish more for myself and it will come, I can feel it in me Irish heart. That heart be sad thinking I won't be there for Fey on her glorious wedding day. So, Mum, sew a fine dress for yourself and kiss her for me.

Your loving daughter,
Agnes

Miss Agnes Logan
The Breakers
Domestic Mail
Ochre Point Avenue
Newport, Rhode Island
USA

August 20, 1905

Dear Agnes,

Well I said my "I dos" and James and I are settled in a fine cottage on the Ballygar Road, not far from the pharmacy. James prefers he be close to his shop. T'was a fine day we had with Father Shea presiding and our friends and family in fine spirits dancin' to the fiddles in the Fitzpatrick's barn. Even James got up and did a jig and he cut a fine figure in his handsome wedding suit. My gown was a simple one with lovely Irish lace insets on the bodice and I wore a circlet of wildflowers in me hair. Of course I made sure

Blackie was there sleek as a racehorse prancing along next to our wedding carriage.

We had our wedding night with all those town galoots ringing' bells and carryin' on hootin' and hollerin' until James bribed them with a bottle of Jamison's from the cupboard.

Your lace handkerchief from the shop in Newport is a sweet and thoughtful treasure. I framed it with a note, "From my dear friend Agnes, in Newport, RI, America." James says it is pretentious, but I think it is grand.

I still go out ridin' on Blackie, and have a chuckle on how we named my white horse, you and I, just to be different girls. But, you are different, my fine, brave woman, my dear friend and I miss you terribly. May you be always safe in your adventure.

Your dear friend,
Fey or as they call me now
Mrs. James O'Connell

Mr. and Mrs. John Galvin
Galvin's Emerald Inn
10 Maiden Lane
New York, New York

August 31, 1905

Dear Maureen and John,

I've been in such a state of worry that with the season's end I would be dumped like an old piece of coal to find a meager position in a drafty old house. Then Mrs. Holmes, that pasty, haughty housekeeper called me in. I thought I was getting the boot, but was told the Countess Barbara was staying on. She said to stop standing there like a stupid girl for there was much to do before leaving for New York! Oh, Maureen, there is truly a saint on my shoulder who is sending me back to the city with the towers in the sky.

Well, you can imagine, though the servants here just follow orders, I surely needed to know more about the packing. At bath time, I asked the Countess in my most servile voice if I needed to prepare her trunk for New York. "Oh Agnes," she smiled, "I am so happy Mrs. Holmes agreed to let you come with me." Now, that was a shocker, I'll say.

So, the Count went off to his castle, the Countess is taking me on a journey to New York. I've so much to learn. My friend, Eileen, Mrs. Astor's lady's maid, says the New York mansion is and on 57th Street and Fifth Avenue. Chipper and me did not get that far in our travels, but I'm thinking that's where the rich are hanging their hats.

With luck, I'll be having tea in your cozy kitchen in a bit.

Your grateful friend,
Agnes

NEW YORK CITY 1905 – 1907

The Winds of Change

Mrs. Patrick Logan
Ros Leana Farm
Ballygar, County Galway
Ireland

December 15, 1905

Dear Mum,

My head was spinning with all the excitement of the Christmas season here. The city does dress up in glory with festooned trees and candle lights and in certain spots the electric light, a truly amazing invention. Countess Barbara had roses in her cheeks from the cold as we made our way from one fancy shop to another, me wondering at the displays of jewels and silks and bon bons. Now, Mum, bon bons are just chocolates, but in the French style. I'm the one, now, puttin' on airs.

It's been a lively time but I fear the tide may be turnin'. Countess Barbara postponed her return to Hungary, despite the protestations of Count Josef. Her wish to remain through the spring may be thwarted, I fear. When his letters arrived the bloom on her cheeks faded.

The Vanderbilt's mansion is too big for its boots if you ask me, taking up a whole block and towering over its neighbors. It be a cold and drafty place that keeps us servants fetching this and that and lighting fires to keep the masters warm. Still, Mrs. Vanderbilt had her Christmas ball. What a to do! My friend, Eileen, was all abuzz with the gossip. Seems they be always snubbing each other, but Mrs. Astor's daughter was all agog to go to the ball. Maybe she thought she'd meet some fancy count. So, the lady herself, Mrs. Astor, arrives at the door dressed like a fur baron's wife to pay her respects. That she is. I'm in the know. Their money is all from poor dead animals. You'd think it was the Queen of England herself. So, they came to the ball, herself laden down with emeralds and diamonds. Eileen was there, of course, as was I. Eileen was scuttlin' around all night, holding this and holding that and standing guard over the diamonds. I do say I was thrilled at the gowns and music and, yes, some of the gentlemen, but kept meself sedate and proper.

On my day off I am much less proper, rushing about to my next adventure. I must have been a tinker in some life for I love wandering around, pokin' my nose where it shouldn't be. When I can I visit Maureen and John and me friend Chipper who gleefully escorts me 'round the sites. Chipper found me a bike to use and up Fifth Avenue we went, getting a bit dusty but passing those fancy stone mansions along the way, with the carriages all lined up in front and a footman at the ready. Chipper says now that I live uptown in a mansion of all things, soon I'll be too fancy for the downtown galoots.

Oh, Mum, then we came to a sainted place, The Cathedral of St. Patrick, our patron saint. The spires rose high above the city, pointing to heaven. Chipper, who knows everything, said it took twenty years to build and I believe it. He doffed his hat, took me hand and said, "Come, let's say a prayer." Well, I was sure the likes of us would be shooed away, but he said the Cathedral is where all New Yorkers come in gladness and sadness. Inside, there are white marble columns and beautiful stained glass windows and statues of the saints. I genuflected, blessed myself and said a fine prayer for all of us, and of course, meself for surely I need the help. I do want more for meself, and something deep inside me says I will find it here, maybe with St. Patrick's help.

I must go now, but I see you by the hearth, wrapped in your shawl as the winter winds blow from the sea, and long for your loving arms. My head is straight, Mum, and I will soldier on with your sacrifice and love my beacons of hope.

Your loving daughter,
Agnes

Miss Agnes Logan
c/o Galvin's Emerald Inn
10 Maiden Lane
New York, New York
USA

January 2, 1906

Dear Sis,

It's sure not easy keeping' up with you and your travelin' ways, cavorting' in New York City with the likes of the idle rich. Me head and me knuckles are raw. Me head from all the studyin' I've been crammin' into it, and me knuckles from workin' on the docks to keep me in knickers. They have us lads in a dormitory, fifty strong and no nonsense to be had. I am a saint, can you believe? Sure, the urge comes upon me to have a pint now and then, but I keep my wits and study the math and the blueprints and all manner of amazin' tools that are used on the new steel ships.

It's school three days and work at the shipyard three days, poundin' bolts into steel the thickness of a castle wall. The company is named Harland and Wolff, not Irish for sure, but they have the money for me trainin' so I'd work for a Chinaman if that be the case. It's amazin' to me that I got one semester under me belt, and if I continue doing well I will advance. Up the ladder, sis, up the ladder, hangin' on like me young self on the roof of the barn.

I miss the folks and the comfort of the farm especially on the cold nights when the wee blankets we have don't cover the chill. Father Shea has arranged to get me grades and although he can be priestly kind I would not want his wrath, so I blur my eyes and freeze me fingers and study through the night.

Is it cold now in the big city and do you get to go out and about on that amazin' trolley car? Wouldn't it be grand if they had a school for you to use that fine brain of yours? We are in times of change. I see it every day in the excitement of this Belfast, growing with leaps like the frogs in the meadow.

Keep safe and watch out for Chinamen.

Your best brother,
Charlie

Miss Agnes Logan
Hotel Astor
100 West 44th Street
New York, New York

January 15, 1906

Dear Agnes,

I have heard from Maureen that you may be seeking employment come June as the Countess is finally going home to her husband. The staff arrived while the Vanderbilt's are visiting in Europe and you were not among them. It is not my intention to interfere, but John had a word with Mrs. Holmes and you have proven yourself to her for which I compliment you. There will be a lady's maid position open again this season for the visiting guests of the Vanderbilt's, for which you are qualified.

It does concern me that you have not spoken of this to Mrs. Holmes whilst in New York, though I hear you are with the Countess at a hotel preparing her trunks for her trip back to Hungary. That is perfectly understandable.

It is commendable that you have done so well, but I would not wish you to be cast adrift so early in your employment. I feel a sense of responsibility toward you and feel we formed a bond last summer. Perhaps a note to Mrs. Holmes will resolve this dilemma.

With affection and hope that you will be here soon.

Norah

Mr. Charles Logan
Belfast College of Technology
Dormitory Three
300 Victoria Blvd.
Belfast, Northern Ireland
United Kingdom

February 1, 1906

Dear Charlie,

This America is a great country and I am just bustin' to tell you my news. I thought I might be in beggar's clothes when my lady, the Countess, was summoned back to Hungary as my summer work was not in place. It is true I am but her servant, but she cannot hide her unhappiness and I dry her tears and she opens her heart. Some days we walk along together looking in the shops on the fancy Fifth Avenue and we sometimes stop in St. Patrick's for a quick prayer. She says I be like a confidante (another French word) and friend and she will never forget all the kindness I have shown her. Charlie, since her husband, Count Josef booked her passage on the SS Deutschland leavin' next week, I thinks she be like a damaged robin I would nurture in the palm of me hand.

So, there I am, preparing her tea and she says to sit with her and talk. She is leaving him and summoned her father from Boston to come and get her for she is weak and sad and fearful and needs her Dah.

Himself arrives, a fine Boston Irishman with fortunes from the steamships. Well, she was always just the Countess to me, and little did I even know her given name was Barbara Farrell. It goes to show I have much to learn. And Charlie, so I did. The Commander, as he is called, arrived like the wind of Western Ireland, filling the room with a strong, sturdy presence. I did a bit of a curtsy. He said, "No bowing to me, young lady, I am in your debt." He called for tea and whiskey and we sat by the hearth.

The Countess seemed to get her spine back, for she stopped her moanin' and had a shot of whisky. Took it straight down. T'was then I saw that Irish flash in her hazel eyes, like her spirit was restored to its proper place. The Commander went on about some new-fangled invention called the wireless that would get the message to the Count that she would not be on the SS Deutschland, and he doubted very much if the Hungarian army would be indeed invading us.

When she took my hand, and said I must come with them to Boston, I was relieved I would be spared finding a proper place for meself. It was then that all the saints heard my prayers in the most miraculous way. The Commander said, "We owe you, dear Agnes, more than a life of service." It was like the light of a rainbow shone down and I grasped it, pushing me fears away. I spoke of how I wished to better meself and he simply said, "I believe there is a way."

He spoke of his friend, Thomas Hunter, who founded a college for women, a free college in the city. He told me of Mr. Hunter's vision and his hope for all women of any race or religion to learn and improve themselves. He said the Hunter College has a school to become a teacher. But I am leaping ahead of myself. It be that Mr. Hunter is so fair that one is only accepted on merit, but the Commander will find what I must do for the entrance exams. Charlie, me heart was beating so fast it was clogging me eardrums and I thought surely I was hearin' things. He said it would be a good beginning for me and we must put first things first. I was so flustered I just shook me head like a bobble doll. Barbara said she would help me prepare for the exams, and he said, "Grand, just grand. Now, my two lovely lasses, we'll celebrate at Delmonico's."

She twirled me around the room, said to stop calling her countess, and had another shot of whiskey. Charlie, just like you said, times are changin' and we be too. Soon spring will be comin' and the flowers will be up and I pray your cold nights are behind you and the sun shines on ye back.

Your loving sister,
Agnes

Mrs. John Galvin
41 Dixon Street
Newport, Rhode Island

February 3, 1906

Dear Norah,

Your kind thoughts for my well-being are much appreciated. I be fine, though a bit flummoxed by the events of this past week. The Countess is leaving her husband and will not be returning to Hungary. I will continue to be in service. She will be employing me in Boston and then in her summer home in a place called Cape Cod.

Now I do not wish to be worryin' you, dear Norah, but through the kindness of her father, Commander Farrell, I will be taking exams for entrance into the normal school at Hunter College. This be a fine chance to better meself and I be puttin' my energies to this task.

My feelin' is the news of her divorce will be showin' up in the society pages any day now, for she will be missin' that boat for sure. Time will only tell if I shall continue in service and see you and your lovely boys.

With love and affection for all your kindness and help to this young Irish traveler.

Love,
Agnes

Ms. Agnes Logan
The Astor Hotel
c/o Farrell
100 W. 43rd Street
New York, New York
USA

February 15, 1906

My darlin' Agnes,

We just came in from Mass and our prayers for you and Charlie. The two of ya are such jack rabbits, jumpin' faster than my weak Irish knees can keep up. 'Tis true I be not in my dotage, but I surely did leave my prime somewhere in a potato field, I fear.

I had a note from Norah and she be concerned that you be havin' some foolish ideas with this school thing and you'll be a beggar soon. It did get me bristles up for I be knowin' you better than the likes of her.

Fey not a year married and the old hags are agin' cacklin' away there be no baby. She be a bit listless, I fear, for James do not like her ridin' that horse of hers. No doubt you will be exchangin' letters for she misses you to the bone. For me now 'tis Sunday, so I'll be cookin' a salmon Mike pulled from the river at down. Pa is readin' in his rocker and the boys are headin' for a bit of horse-play on the green. God and the saints be with you my brave girl.

Your loving Mum
Rose

Mrs. James O'Connell
21 Ballygar Road
Ballygar, Gounty Galway
Ireland

February 20, 1906

Dear Fey,

I see you in your Sunday best, strolling with James and smiling at the old biddies while you'd rather be riding in the breeze or dipping your toes in the river. My time is as tight as a corset on one of them fat opera singers but it's no excuse for not writin' to you.

I wouldn't worry me Mum, but this is a fretful time. 'Tis true I have Maureen and John who embrace me with their kindness, and my friend, Eileen, Mrs. Astor's lady's maid. When we can and are in the same city, we sit by the ocean or the river and speak of home. But, if I could reach out and touch you, we would be under the Rose of Sharon tree sharin' the joys and fears of our lives. I would be tellin' you the time is near to take the exams for the Normal School at Hunter College, a miracle itself. Barbara Farrell and her father, the Commander, stayed on in New York after she dumped the count, perhaps she had to catch her breath before she went home, but he's buzzin' in and out every day, conducting business. Barbara has been tutoring me and improving my writing and spelling. No dropped "g's" she says.

I've been doing the math, too, but I fear it will do me in. I am more for the words than the numbers. Commander Farrell brought me history books on America and my brain is swollen' with names and dates. It is truly amazing how George Washington led the people to freedom from the Brits. We could use one of him.

Now, I hope you and James are faring well and you have made some friends with the other young married ladies. Wouldn't it be grand if you could visit New York, and Chipper and me could show you the town? We could send James off for a pint with John Galvin and have a girl day, following the breeze from the Hudson River.

Fey, you know me. You know I show a strong outside even when I'm quivering like jelly inside. I did so with Maureen and John when I first arrived, a ragged bundle of fear. I do so with terrifying Mrs. Holmes at the Vanderbilt estate. I pretended I knew what I was doing when I first met Countess Barbara and when the Commander appeared, taking me in hand. Now I must march into that learned institution of Hunter College and be tested in Grammar, Composition and Spelling, United States History and Arithmetic. I'll wear my neatest dress and shine my shoes, tie back my hair in a braid, hold my head high and pretend you are next to me, never doubting my quest as you did when I left you, my dear, wonderful Fey.

Your loving friend,
Agnes

Mrs. Patrick Logan
Ros Leana Farm
Ballygar, County Galway
Ireland

February 22, 1906

Dear Mum,

I sent a letter to Fey bringin' her up to date on my adventures, and now I'm thinking I might be too full of meself. Great kindness has been shown to me and I must keep my wits to be a worthy one. The Farrells have returned to Boston and I will be joinin' them there after the outcome of my exams. Be it pass or fail I be needing employment. So, Norah need not worry I be a beggar. Mum, Norah has been very kind to me in her no-nonsense way. She be strict in her ways but she has a fine husband, home and children and need not worry of her place in life.

For now, I'm with Maureen and John who have carved out a little cubby for me on the third floor near the linen closet. It's fine with a lovely cedar smell seeping through the thin wall. They are truly saints to take me up like this.

Now that I'm not living in some ritzy hotel, I'm enjoying some home cooking, though that salmon makes me long for home and our Sunday dinners. So, dear Mum, all be well for now.

Love to Pa and the boys.

Your loving daughter,
Agnes

Miss Agnes Logan
c/o Galvin's Emerald Inn
10 Maiden Lane
New York, New York
USA

February 25, 1906

Dear Sis,

We be movin' up in the world, you and me, the likes of us! You should see me muscles, Sis. I shot up an inch or two and all that sweatin' has put me pecs lookin' like a sailor. The foreman at the shipyard took me in hand, said I was one of his best workers and I had a brain. Jeez, I'm gettin' praise in this Protestant place. Anyway, I am promoted to supervisor in one of the weldin' galleys, so my back ain't achin' so much.

Father Shea is never far behind me grades, checkin' up like a proper patron. No complaints, but I miss Mum, especially when I know she is strugglin' with loneliness for us. Mum says you be taken the test any day now for that special women's school. You got the brains no doubt, with all your learnin', even if Sister Dominic said you were a wicked girl for your sass. You'll be needin' it in that America.to stand up and be counted. I guess I will light a candle in a Protestant church. Don't tell Farther Shea.

Your best brother,
Charlie

Mrs. Patrick Logan
Ros Leana Farm
Ballygar, County Galway
Ireland

March 15, 1906

Dear Mum,

I had a note from Charlie wishing me luck on my test. He be a busy lad, but seems to be thriving.

So, I did it. I took the test for the Hunter College. John and Maureen, in all their kindness, took me all the way uptown in their horse and buggy so I wouldn't get meself covered with dust on my bike. Oh Mum, what a sight to see, this huge brick building with a stone staircase leading up to the entrance, all softened by lovely vines of wisteria, like arms urging me forward. Maureen turned me around and smoothed my skirt and jerkin then gave me a little pat and up I went.

I was to meet a Miss Wadleigh and there she was, a very tall, large woman with the most piercing eyes I ever saw. I entered a grand hall and she led me to a classroom. Soon the room was filled with young ladies of every color, size and shape you ever did see. It was like the world opened up in that classroom. She passed out the tests with instructions, folded her arms and kept those piercing eyes on us all as we worked. I was so grateful I had my English and Grammar and Composition. Thank the Lord I was tutored in American History by Countess Barbara for that was an important part of the exam. You know, Mum, me and numbers don't always get along, but I struggled through and think I may have made the grade. Soon I will hear. Keep those candles burnin'.

All my love,
Agnes

Miss Agnes Logan
c/o Galvin Emerald Inn
10 Maiden Lane
New York, New York
USA

March 29, 1906

My dear Friend Agnes,

My heart would sing if James and me could do such a thing as travel to America. But, he is a bit tight with the pence and keeps serious books on the comings and goings of our income. He says he'll be buildin' a bigger cottage for us soon with room with little ones. No baby be comin' yet and I be healthy as a horse though James gives me a tonic for me blood or something; him bein' a pharmacist.

It's the way here, Aggie, to be bringin' children into the world. I am so proud of you, my friend. You were always the bravest and the brightest and never let a soul put you in your place, though we both know times when you deserved it.

Mrs. O'Hara, who thinks who she is bein' the Mayor's wife, was raisin' her bushy grey brows when I told her of you comin' up in the world. Must be rememberin' when you scared her bloomers off nearly clippin' her on your bike.

My life is a quiet one and I keep a handsome home for us. Can you imagine me bakin' meat pies and scones and sewin' up curtains? James has his soft side with me though he can be stern. He didn't want me ridin' Blackie now that I be a proper married lady. Well there are horsewomen all over Ireland prancing around those rings, I said. Then I teared up about me best friend bein' on the other side of the ocean. I was grand, I'll say. I take him out and ride as I please, waitin' for the chance to mud up Mrs. O'Hara.

I stop by to see your Mum at least once a week, and she showed me your letter. We shared our amazement at your courage for marchin' into that great school and taking' them tests. Days when I'm ridin' Blackie I rein up in the meadow and lie in the grass lookin' at the sky. It is where I send my love and prayers to you, my faithful and far way friend.

Your loving friend,
Fey

Hunter College
625 Park Avenue
New York, NY

Miss Agnes Logan
c/o Galvin Emerald Inn
10 Maiden Lane
New York, New York

April 1, 1906

Dear Miss Logan,

This is to advise that you have successfully completed the entrance requirements for admission to the Freshman Class of Hunter College.

I am pleased to welcome you to the 1906 Fall Semester. Orientation will be on Monday, September 7, 1906. At that time, you will be given your course schedule and a tour of the college.

Since this is a free institution of learning when you receive your syllabus the books will be provided to you.

I will be available to assist you with any questions or concerns as you begin your higher education.

Yours truly,
Lydia Wadleigh
Dean

Miss Barbara Farrell
18 Chestnut Street
Beacon Hill
Boston, Massachusetts

April 10, 1906

Dear Barbara,

It is with astonishment and joy I can notify you of my acceptance to Hunter College. The kindness and respect you and the Commander have shown me must be a great trait in this America. Surely the vision of himself, Thomas Hunter, fills the open halls of the school.

I await your word as to my employment with you in Boston, if that is still as you wish. If you have had a change of heart perhaps I can find a wee job for myself, maybe at Macy's or that Bloomingdales if Maureen will still have me.

But enough of me. You must be shuffling invitations for the new season now that you are rid of tutoring me which was a great gift I can never repay. Though I came to you as your lady's maid and am surely not your social equal, it was grand to see you bright and smiling in the warm embrace of your loving family

Now, I embark on another journey. Seems me feet just keep tappin' along.

Your forever grateful,
Agnes

Miss Agnes Logan
c/o Galvin
10 Maiden Lane
New York, New York

April 15, 1906

Dear Agnes,

We are so pleased you passed the entrance examination, but this is just the first step in a long journey, and one you will not travel alone.

Since I returned home, I have reflected on the tumultuous year that has passed. I have led a privileged life, yet let my good sense was swept away by the trappings of high society. I allowed the false embrace of my own importance lead me to become another heiress who married royalty, a grievous mistake.

When you first came to me in Newport I was burdened with sadness, a rich young woman surrounded by wealth and prestige in a gilded cage. My vision of you was blurred, so caught up in my own needs. On the night of the fireworks when you saw my tears and took my hand, I realized how self-centered I had become.

I saw you then; a young woman of my age, who had come across the ocean to start a new life. But more than that I saw in you a great strength and humanity that left me wanting. It is I who owe you a debt.

You made me realize I have the means and the connections to be useful to society and not be a social dilettante. With my family's blessing I have begun a foundation to help young women such as yourself and you are the first recipient. The Farrell Foundation for Women will provide for your living expenses, including room and board while you are a student at Hunter College.

Education is a precious gift. You should embrace it without fear of how you will live day to day. Daddy and I will arrange all the details for you with the bank when we come for the Newport to New York Regatta in August. I will continue to seek worthy women who need assistance.

I have enclosed a money order for your trip to Boston. I would recommend you take the nine am train on Friday, April 25th from Grand Central Depot at 42nd Street. Something tells me your intrepid friend, Chipper, will assist in getting you to the station. See you then.

Fondly,
Barbara Farrell

Mr. Charles Logan
Belfast College of Technology
Dormitory Three
300 Victoria Blvd.
Belfast, Northern Ireland
United Kingdom

April 30, 1906

Dear Charlie,

So here we be, two bumpkins from the farm, you bein' promoted and me passing my exams!

I marched right up those great stone steps and teased me brain to work. There is a bit of shock to all of it as Barbara Farrell has started a foundation of all things and they are to help me with my expenses. Before I could get me head straight with all this news, I was boardin' the train to Boston where I be now.

Oh, Charlie, 'tis another wonder of the city, The Grand Central Depot. I got me pal, Chipper, the New York explorer, to take me in hand. He grabbed me up at Maureen's and took me to South Ferry where we get on an underground train. Can you believe it? They call it the subway. I was certainly fearful, but hung on to him and in no time, we were there. We arrived at Vanderbilt Avenue and he said it was so named because the Commodore Cornelius built the station. Chipper knows just about everything about this city. Sure, it was a blessing he was with me for the size of it alone would have sent me scurryin' to a corner. Though I be in New York for a bit now, it has so many wonders one can be a bit overcome at times. He took me to the platform for the Boston train. A great arched glass ceiling rose above the tracks, and ladies and gentlemen of all means hustled about. Leave it to him to even know a few of them! Then I was in me cozy seat with me notebook and me book, "The Scarlett Pimpernel", which is an historical novel. I'm reading as much as I can to prepare for my schoolin'.

Barbara had a car waiting for me at the station. A car! I never. The driver gave me a long tan coat to put on and a pair of goggles for me eyes so I would be protected from the "elements." He should have seen me on the boat from Ireland. I guess I have come up in the world.

So here I be in Beacon Hill, a fancy address they be tellin' me, though I should be getting used to livin' with the high class, even though I be on the sidelines. I'm realizin' that you're almost over your first year of studies. We are all so proud of you, and Mum ever grateful for what you send her. Now with the summer comin' she will use it to hire some lad to shovel the barn. God bless and keep those muscles strong.

Your loving sister,
Agnes

Mrs. Patrick Logan
Rose Leana Farm
Ballygar. County Galway
Ireland

June 30, 1906

Dear Mum,

I've been in fine spirits, workin' and enjoying the pleasures of another American city, this Boston. The Boston Tea Party, as it is called, started the American Revolution. Barbara was a fine guide takin' me around and showin' off the city of her birth. Her mum, Loretta Farrell, has a bit of the lace curtain in her, and has been stand offish with the likes of me settlin' in her home on Beacon Hill. Barbara knows I'd be against takin' her charity, so I continue to be in her employ as a lady's maid much to the delight of Loretta who's always braggin' around about havin' a servant to iron her undies. So the other day after my studies, she calls on me to prepare her trunk for we are goin' to Cape Cod. Now I'm thinkin' that sounds like a smelly place, but what do I know of the nooks and crannies of this land.

Barbara said not to worry. It's their summer home right on the ocean and not fancy at all and her mother is just puttin' on airs again. But, Mum, wait till you hear. We sailed there in the Commander's yacht, the Norah B, named after his beloved mother.

My sea legs were tested for sure as we sailed along in the wind, flyin' like a seabird. And the home is a simple one, something called a saltbox for its odd shape, but cheery and comfortable for its views of the ocean. I feel right at home here, and go for long walks along the dunes and go bicycling with Barbara. Blessings abound.

Your loving daughter,
Agnes

Miss Agnes Logan
c/o Farrell
32 Dune Road
Hyannsis, Massachusetts
USA

July 20, 1906

My darlin' Agnes,

'Tis a blessin you be near the sea for it do fill your heart with joy. I be sharin' your adventures, but we be needin' a map to place where you be. Well, the whole of Ireland could be fittin' into a corner of the great USA.

I be holdin' me head high with you goin' to a fine institution of learnin, and tellin' of your scholarship. Now that's a cause for celebration and Pa and the boys had a pint or two, raising their glasses to yer.

Charlie be spendin' the summer in Belfast workin' on those ships. Although this be a small country compared to the United States, he won't be comin' home, but sent us some money notes to help with the farm. Father Shea made the trip to Belfast as he can stay at a rectory there, and he said Charlie's frame has filled out and he is brown from the sun.

Now the summer days be long, with the twilight at eleven and the soft breeze blowin' across the fields. Sittin' in me rocker as these shinin' days wane, I miss you till me heart is sore.

Your loving mum,
Rose

Mrs. Patrick Logan
Ros Leana Farm
Ballygar, County Galway
Ireland

August 15, 1906

Dearest Mum,

If St. Agnes is indeed the patron saint of young women she has worked a miracle for me, her namesake. As it is I'm am breathless with joy and thanks for the fates that have led me to this grand place of learning I came back to the cedar scented room at Maureen's to await Barbara and the Commander who said we need to do the paper work for the foundation gift. I truly expected to be finding a wee job to keep me in hairpins and bloomers and give something to Maureen and John. Oh, Mum, this may be a thought so strange to you as it was to me. I met them at the Astor Hotel. Maura gave me a lovely shawl with a fancy fringe to wear and Chipper insisted to take me on the trolley. He was all agog at meeting those rich folks, he said. Barbara explained they would take care of my expenses and pay rent for lodging as long as I kept the grades. Then I signed some papers and they hailed a fancy cab and took me to the Morgan Stanley bank. It seems I now have an account. Can you believe such a thing? Me, Agnes Logan, with an account.

Then the Commander said there is a lovely boarding house near the school and that Thomas Hunter sometimes arranged for students to live there. It is not so proper here for a young lady to be on her own, and this is a respectable home with no hanky panky. Barbara burst out laughing and said I wouldn't have time for any hanky panky. Well, that's for sure for my flirtin' has been getting rusty since I set foot in America.

Maureen and John are completely flummoxed by all this attention I be getting. John has sent word that he wishes to meet the Commander before I leave as he feels it is his duty to see I will be safe. Something tells me that these two big, commanding Irishmen will like the stride and strength of each other.

Oh Mum, my semester will start soon. I wonder if I be in a beautiful bubble that a single pin will burst as I scamper to right myself from my pride and folly.

All my love to Pa and Pat and Mike.

Your loving daughter,
Agnes

Miss Agnes Logan
c/o Galvin's Emerald Inn
10 Maiden Lane
New York, New York

September 15, 1906

Dear Agnes,

I be back in New York now with the Astor's on Fifth Avenue. I can but barely believe since we met on the boat to Newport how your life has taken such a turn. It is an amazin' to me that you find the strength to move on. Five years now I've been waitin' on the wealthy, but Mrs. Astor is a kind employer and I be doin' okay with this life.

This winter she will be takin' me with her to Tuscon, Arizona of all places and I think I'll be meetin' some of those Indians. So, in my own way I have an adventure to look forward to.

When we both get settled it would be so grand to spend an afternoon together as I wish we can remain friends.

Fondly,
Eileen

Mrs. Patrick Logan
Ros Leana Farm
Ballygar, County Galway
Ireland

September 30, 1906

Dear Mum,

Oh, now, you should see me in my lovely little room in this place called Rose Hall. It is called a brownstone here in New York. It has what they call a stoop here, and it is brownstone, maybe that is why, but I must find out. It is a narrow building with four floors of small, but tidy rooms. One enters a vestibule (another new word) of the brightest black and white marble. Off that is a dining room and a kitchen where meals are prepared. We girls have an evening bite. Mrs. Rose (after you I think) is so kind so lets us fix a spot of tea if we like. But, Mum, the real magic of this place is the yard off the kitchen filled with little benches and trees. It is a sweet place to hide from the clamor of the city.

The scholarship I received from the Farrell Foundation has been a great blessing. If I were working and schooling at the same time, I think I would be a scrawny shadow of myself, biting me nails and tearing out me hair. There isn't a day goes by I don't bless myself as I head up those grand steps for my classes. Each day begins with an assembly of the student body. There is a reading, choral singing, and a brief homily from President Hunter himself. He is of striking appearance with a shock of black hair and a twinkle in his eye. It is his habit to visit the classrooms and get to know the students which is of great benefit to us all.

I do love my English and Literature, Music and even the Science course, but have a bit of a strain with the Mathematics and getting me Irish tongue around French. Just think, Mum, when the day comes I can see your beautiful face again, I can parlee-vous to the likes of Mrs. O'Hara, my nose in the air as I wave my French perfume scented hanky. Won't it be grand!

Your loving daughter,
Agnes

Miss Eileen Burns
c/o Astor
2100 Fifth Avenue
New York, New York

October 15, 1906

Dear Eileen,

How wonderful to hear from you. I had a different summer this year being in that Cape Cod place, and truly missed our bike rides and visits to our lovely cove. It is true I am a student at Hunter College and a bit overwhelmed by it all, though I do my best to keep my balance and my brain from tipping over in such a heady atmosphere. The students are from many races and religions, part of a broader world that is an education in itself. Some of the girls' work, mostly in a family business, like the Chinese Laundry and Persian rug importers, and they live with their parents and siblings. My friend, Aliza, has a brilliant brother in medical school here who helps her with the sciences. I've been to her home above the carpet store. Tis another world, it is, with chimes and incense and amazing sparkling lamps. Her mom has a red dot on her head. She does.

Now isn't it exciting you have a grand trip to the wild west to look towards. That will surely be a wonderful adventure traveling across this great continent. Perhaps we can find a wee bit of time before you leave for a cup of tea and some Irish girl talk.

With fond regards,
Agnes

Miss Agnes Logan
Rose Hall
320 West 65th Street
New York, New York

April 21, 1907

Dear Sis,

We be movin' up in the world, you and me, the likes of us! I be out of the dorm this being my second year and share a room with four others. Good lads, a mixed bag includin' one bloomy from Liverpool. No politics here, just five worn brains and bodies lookin' for a better life. Can ya believe it? My advisor here, a Prof. Begley, he of the thinned veined hands and drooping nose, says they'll be needin' design engineers and me math is good enough. Says I got the gumption to be an engineer. Tip yer bonnet to me, old girl, swaggerin' along bloody Belfast with me nose in the air. Let me tell ya, this here School of Technology is buzzing like a bee drownin' in honey. Somethin' big is in the smelt that spews all day on the docks. Heard said that our bosses, Harlan and Wolff are outfitting the docks to build the biggest ship the world has ever known. Now that sounds like a lot of boastin' to me. All us lads are waitin' for some news. We be workin' more on buildin' what seems like a giant hole then workin' on the ships these days. Oh, sure, somethin' is brewin, but we are just the dummies doin' the work for now.

There not be too much rest here, just school and work, and I miss the farm and Ma and Pa and me big brothers who have all the burdens. I do have a few quid now to make the trip but 'tis a long ride and time to do so is a fight to find. Maybe we can all meet in the middle somewhere, likes the Cliffs of Moher and I can run barefoot on the hills and play ball with Pat and Mike. Mum can breathe in the beauty of the sea and Dah can rest his weary back. Then we'll look across the great Atlantic and wave to you, standin' on the shore in the great New York, a proper teacher of the fine youth of the world.

Your best brother,
Charlie

Mr. Charles Logan
Belfast College of Technology
Dormitory Three
300 Victoria Blvd.
Belfast, Northern Ireland
United Kingdom

May 22, 1907

Dear Charlie,

Now aren't you the one, swaggering on the streets of Belfast, headin' for a fine career and pride in building a ship like no other. I am just finishing up my second semester and it will be a while before I'll be teaching the fine youth of the world, but I be doin' my very best to get there. To me the teachers are brilliant as the sunlight on a fine July day. I do have my own Father Shea, a Miss Wadleigh who says I am a fine student. It is her duty to report to Barbara and Commander Farrell on my progress and I would never let them down.

Though the scholarship takes care of my expenses during the school year I need to earn a pence or two in the interim. I thought I'd be a lady's maid in the summer if that was possible, and wrote to Norah and Mrs. Holmes. It seems despite my uncomfortable encounters with Mrs. Holmes, she will be in need of a person such as myself for part of the summer season. Norah is thrilled I will be back and I am too, for I have love in my heart for that wonderful family and my Irish cove at the sea.

But now I must get to studyin' for me exams. God Bless.

Your loving sister,
Agnes

Miss Agnes Logan
Rose Hall
320 West 65th Street
New York, New York

June 20, 1907

Dear Agnes,

How wonderful that you have completed your first year of studies so successfully! You are a fine example to those who will follow through my foundation. I was a bit surprised, however, when you decided to return to service this summer though I do understand that soft breezes are far lovelier than the hot dusty streets of New York when the temperature rises. But, I must check myself for thinking of you as a lady of leisure with a summer holiday. It was foolish of me. Once again you have made me realize how deep your struggle is even with the scholarship. Newport is indeed a good choice for you now until you begin your student teaching next year.

My foundation is taking route and I have been interviewing young ladies. I think I may need your counsel as there are obvious gaps in support I need to address. I will be coming to Newport for the Fourth of July celebration. Let's meet then and perhaps I can ease your burden.

With admiration,
Barbara Farrell

JOURNAL 1907-1908

Newport, Rhode Island
July 3, 1907
I've been told by the Headmistress of English, Prof. Chauncey, that I have a gift for the writing, and I must keep a journal to record the observations of me life. I am tearing out me hair, for what does she think I have time for such nonsense. But I suppose I need to practice proper writing if I am ever to teach it correctly.

So, I be in service again here at the Vanderbilts, and Barbara was not too pleased at first. What is she thinking, that I'd be traipsing around New York like some high-born woman stopping in the shops for a bit of tea? Barbara is here for the big Fourth of July to-do, and I be serving Mrs. Stanley of those Stanley Steamer people. Now that one is a sight to behold, so fulsome I get all sweated up pulling her girdle ties. Barbara is much lighter in spirit now that she dumped the Count, and is flitting around like the heiress she is. I'm thinking I should have stayed put in Rose Hall, eking out a living in Macy's or somewhere, for although I'm happy seeing Norah and the family, or going for a bike ride with Eileen, I'm not feeling meself. Maybe the whiff of entitlement sent me spinning.

Barbara popped into my room the other night, looking around to make sure that that no one saw her before she settled in. Now that did bother me, lest I forget who I be. Then she took my hands and smiled and said she was sorry for being such a silly girl this year. I held up my head as I do when I'm a bit put off and said I was doing my best to keep her faith in me. Well, it seems she needs my help, for she didn't understand how really hard it can be for a person like myself to find her way, even with the scholarship. When I finish my duties here and she returns from Cape Cod in August, I'll be heading to Boston to help her decide on another young woman for her foundation award. Oh, I would love it to be Eileen, but she seems connected to the bones of Mrs. Astor.

We will see.

I'm tired and still have to iron the tent of a dress for the ball tomorrow night, and I must start reading Charles Dickens for next semester. Seems he wrote a lot of books. Father in Heaven, give peace and patience to this restless girl. I'll light a candle to Mother Mary at St. Augustine's on Sunday, for she gives me strength.

July 4, 1907

I think I have fallen into a well filled with for swirling sparkles, in a tumult of emotions as my heart races through me. Around seven o'clock the guests arrived for the ball. Even with the breezes from the portico, the evening was a warm one. Mrs. Stanley kept me fetchin' fresh hankies and ice water for her sweaty body. Barbara was gorgeous in a red satin gown and wore a blue feather in her hair, very American like. She pulled me aside and said there was someone she wanted me to meet. I thought she must be mad, me in my humble muslin trying to keep me hair from popping out in the humidity.

When the music started I could barely keep from tappin' me feet as the swirling dancers flitted around me like a carousel. It was then I saw Barbara dancing with a tall gentleman in a white naval uniform. He was like a prince from some fairy tale, so straight and lean; his black hair short but with a wave to it. They were laughing, and when he bent his head to hear her I thought my heart would stop for he looked up straight at me, his eyes a blazing blue and I felt like a rag picker in this grand company of swells.

As the evening waned and the sky darkened, everyone gathered for the fireworks over the ocean. I thought of how sad Barbara was just a year ago, and how both our lives had changed, though mine was still to be defined. Now she was gaily laughing with the man who took my breath away, and I'm the sad one, I'm thinkin'.

By eleven the carriages returned and the guests departed. Too bad Mrs. Stanley wasn't among them. I helped heave her up the grand staircase as she moaned and groaned about her swollen feet, and thought that maybe I was a foolish girl for thinking I could be in service again. My life had taken an unexpected path and though I never thought myself fearful, I came to the comfort of the known. Now I must keep moving forward, write in my journal, read my books and be bright and ready for what comes next.

So, when the clamor died down I took off my shoes and walked through the damp grass to the edge of the cliffs to think. The brightness of the moon led a path across the ocean to my perch on the rocks. It was so perfect I blessed myself, I did, and said a thankful prayer for the beauty and the peace. But my quiet moment was interrupted by a voice: a low, soft voice.

"I believe I've stumbled upon the elusive and beautiful Agnes Logan."

Now who is this eedjit I thought, and turned around. It was him, the prince! I was frozen in place like a wicked witch had put a curse on me. He crouched down beside me.

"Christian Farrell, at your service."

I gathered the few wits I had and managed to croak, "Farrell?'

He smiled. I almost swooned right into the sea. He told me he was Barbara's cousin and he knew all about me and her foundation, and was eager to meet me.

"She told me how very special you are, but I had no idea...no idea you would enchant me with one look."

And so, the earth shifted on its axis.

Father in heaven, give peace and patience to this restless girl.

July 5, 1907
A quiet day. The guests were in a restful mood from the festivities which was a good thing for I was in a bit of a dither from the night before and my encounter with Christian Farrell. I keep replaying it in me head; the moonlight, his charming way, and how he put me at ease, though me heart was thumping in my chest. I did say, holding me head high, if he knew so much about me I was surely at a disadvantage for I had no idea why he was chasin' me down. He said he was a Lieutenant in the United States Navy, a graduate of the Military Academy in Annapolis. His dad and the Commander are brothers, and he and Barbara have always been close first cousins. Well, it seems when he came home on leave and saw the happy change in her, she sang my praises. I said that she and the Commander had given me a great gift and I would not put it to waste.

When we strolled back to the Breakers it was so still, just some soft flickering lanterns leading our way. I hesitated as he opened the door to the ballroom, for I use the servants entrance. Then he bent his head close to mine and whispered, "You will never be a servant." I stopped breathing, I did, and he took my arm and walked me right through the great hall. If this is enchantment I am lost in it, but need to put my head to my next challenge of helping Barbara with her foundation and forget my foolishness.

When I saw her this morning she said Christian left at dawn, for he was on a short leave. It's just as well, for seeing him in the light of day would spoil the magic of last night and I'd be acting like a foolish girl whose brain has turned to mush.

Father in heaven, give peace and patience to this restless girl.

August 1, 1907
Today I said goodbye to Norah and Tom and the boys. Raymond Burns brought me a bouquet of the loveliest flowers and took me to the train to Boston. It is called The Dandy Train, for all the wealthy gentlemen who ride in comfort between Newport and Boston. A person like me pays one American dollar and off I go. I thought I might be in the caboose but the train had pretty wicker seats, and though it was crowded, I managed to get a comfy spot by the window. It was a charming ride along Narragansett Bay.

As I watched the sailboats skipping on the bay I began to understand that though there are many threads pulling me to and fro, I do like the challenge of a new adventure. Once again Barbara had a car waiting for me at the station. The chauffer elegantly escorted me. I held me head high and spine straight, thank you very much.

When I got to their townhouse, the Commander greeted me with a warm hug, and a gentle reprimand that I was not to be in service again. Now, that is all well and good, but I sometimes think they've gone daft. I am no debutant. Then Barbara called for tea. She said we were reviewing the goals and objectives of the foundation for I had a better grasp on what a young woman of limited needs required. Its seems I'm always spinnin' around. One day I'm tying up stays on the fat one and the next I'm some kind of consultant. That's what she says I am, a consultant of all things, and I will be paid.

After tea she walked me upstairs to the same darling room I stayed in last year. I do love it. I do. There is flowered blue paper on the walls, a cozy rocker near the fire, and soft white curtains that float with the breeze from the St. Charles River. I could see she was bustin' to tell me something for her eyes were all sparkling. I'm thinking she must be in love, for sure. Then she closed the door and opened the drawer of a little side table and retrieved a letter. "Someone left this for you," she laughed.

I sat down on the rocker and held a crisp white envelope with the name Agnes Logan written in black ink. Barbara said she'd leave me be and left. Now I'm thinking it's some terrible news from home or Maura and John in New York, but then Barbara was smiling. She surely knows something I don't. I opened it.

July 15, 1907

Dear Miss Logan,

I am trying to be a proper gentleman. Since we met so briefly I reserve the right to just say Agnes. Our meeting or my "chasin' you down", as you so aptly put it felt like a perfect moment that I treasure. You have destroyed my concentration and left me thinking of our midnight stroll as I try to prepare for my mission on the USS Connecticut. I am waiting for my orders.

I will be out to sea for a year or even more, depending on the commitment of the United States Navy which I proudly serve. If that were not the case, it would be my intention to properly court you, with permission of course, from your extended family on Maiden Lane. The Commander has a great fondness for John Galvin, and when he is in New York he makes a point to visit with him.

Since this is not imminently possible, you would do me a great service by writing to me while I am away. The Navy has arrangements to distribute mail whilst we are at sea. Barbara tells me you are a conscientious writer to your friends and family, and it would be an honor to be included.

May every day be filled with the beauty, joy and gifts you so delightfully bring to the world.

With admiration,
Christian Farrell

I read it about a dozen times. My cheeks are burning just at the thought of him. My beauty, joy and gifts! I thought I was a sorry sight that night, sitting on those cliffs in me bare feet, all sweaty from the demands of the huge one. I guess I still have a lot to learn about myself. I heard a tap at the door and Barbara came in, smiling and giggling. It seems he asked her to give me his letter, and she was just dying to hear its contents! Said we were two very special people in her life and wasn't it just grand.

Well, I'm not so sure how the likes of him could be taken with a poor Irish lass, but I told her I would write to him as he asked, for after all, he was protecting us out there on that big ship. It's been a day, Prof. Chauncy. Time for some lovely dreams.

August 3, 1907

Dear Lieut. Farrell,

You may call me Agnes, for you have charmed me with your gentlemanly tone. I have never been courted, sir, and wonder if before you go runnin' off all the way downtown to Maiden Lane, that you mention such a thought to me. It seems that the Commander,

John Galvin and Barbara are in cahoots and I am the last to know what is coming next. I just know I will keep moving forward by helping Barbara and starting my second year as a student at Hunter College. My life has been blessed through a series of events that began on that very same cliff in Newport the night Barbara was so sad. It seems that spot has a magic to it, for now I am writing to you, a fine gentleman in the United States Navy who wants to court me.

Soon I will be heading back to Rose Hall in New York to take up residence for my schooling, and you will be defendin' our shores in the middle of the great Atlantic. I will think of you and pray to keep you safe.

God Speed,
Agnes

September 1, 1907

Dear Agnes,

It was my dearest wish that you would correspond with me and I you charmed me once again with your letter. I will be stationed here at Hampton Bays preparing for President Roosevelt has commissioned a fleet of ships to sail around the world, and I will be aboard the USS Connecticut heading for South America. We ship out of Hampton Roads, Virginia in a few weeks. Once I am at sea I fear months will pass without communication. I will write to you whenever I can, and you may get one big bundle of soggy, salty notes one day. But it is my intention that you remember me, and not go running off with some slick New Yorker who will charm you with champagne and carriage rides.

How can it be you have never been courted? When I first spied you in the ballroom I thought I would be fighting for a chance just to spend a few moments with you. Now here I am going all he way around the world with hopes you will still be free on my return.

With my best to Barbara and the Commander, I remain your admiring,

Christian

P.S. Do call me Christian.

September 15, 1907

Dear Christian,

It is a wonderful thing to go around the world. Imagine the sights you will see. I have but come across the ocean, and it was an arduous journey, so I may be envious of your exciting travels, but not of the rough seas.

No sir, I have not been properly courted, but I do have a gentlemen friend in New York who takes me around to all the great sights and smells and sounds of the city. His name is Chipper, a rascal of sorts who travels free on the electric cars, knows all the important councilmen, and carries me books after school. I have a great fondness for him.

In fact, he was waiting for me after school today, his hair all slicked back, a big smile on his face and a stick of licorice in his hand. He is rather like that character in Dickens, the Artful Dodger, but he does not steal. Oh, yes, I have been reading Charles Dickens as required by Prof. Chauncey. But, Christian, to put you at ease, Chipper is sixteen.

I'm feeling a sense of comfort in school this year and it was lovely to see my classmates again. Now I may not be travelin' around the world, but I do know some Chinese and Indian people. As a second-year student I am to be available to help the newcomers. Each morning when the great Thomas Hunter speaks before class, it is a joy to see the wonder in their faces. I surely must have looked like a bloomin' idiot when I first walked into these halls. Truth be told, I was terrified.

Staying at Rose Hall is through the kindness of Barbara and the Commander and surely eases the worry of dear Maureen and John Galvin to know I won't be snatched off the street like some waif.

I will think of you in your smart white uniform saluting our great president, Theodore Roosevelt.

God Speed,
Agnes

October 10, 1907

Dear Agnes,

I hear the lilt in your voice in your letters, the soft witty gift of the Irish It is almost as if you are here beside me. That is not to be for a long time. Today we put to sea, passing in review before President Roosevelt, who was flying his flag on the presidential yacht, Mayflower. It was a sight to see. Rails were manned with officers who were decked in special full dress, cocked hats, epaulets, white satin-lined swallow tail coats and gold-striped trousers. It was cold on that deck and we have just begun. Our captain, Rear Admiral Robley D. Evans, leads with a strong hand and a sharp eye so we are all on our best behavior. I felt proud to be a part of this historic event.

I was fortunate to receive your letter before we set sail. When I heard of your fine gentleman, my heart sank, for I thought for sure my chances were dimmed, but you have teased me, Miss Logan. You are irrepressible and I should have known that by the sparkle in your eyes. Please spare me from despair.

I have heard of Thomas Hunter. He is a fine example of an Irish gentleman and a great visionary. It is good to know you are safe at Rose Hall, but I doubt anyone would think of you as a waif.

It is very late, the light is dim, so I will say goodnight, dear Agnes.

With admiration
Christian

December 5, 1907

Dear Christian,

And now you are off to see this world. I rushed to the news sellers to get the paper and saw a picture of the President and those fancy dignitaries all saluting you as you sailed away. How grand! I received a note from Barbara, and she said the Commander was aboard the Mayflower with the President. He must be so proud of you, his beloved nephew. It seems he even knows your first port of call. Now don't go thinkin' I know all that navy lingo. I learned it from Barbara, I did. So, then you're to be in a place called Trinidad.

There is a grand globe of the world in Prof. Higgins geography room and I study it, running my fingers around the map following your fleet. The Professor has been helpful in guiding my fingers to the Straits of Magellan out to the Pacific Ocean. He said it is a dangerous journey in treacherous waters. My thoughts turn fearful when I hear such things, even though we have barely met and I am but a corrrespondent to a gentleman far away from home.

Indeed, it is a cold December. The wind off the river here blows fiercely, and it is a great relief I have but a few streets to walk. Even my gentleman friend has not been so faithful with his licorice and book-carrying.

The school has high expectations of us ladies, and the studying is intense, but my French is much better this year, thanks to Prof. LeBlanc, a thin, prissy, gentleman who seems to have forgotten how to give a smile.

Here's but hoping this note reaches you in that Trinidad place.

God Speed,
Agnes

March 15, 1908

Dear Agnes,

Your letter reached me in San Diego and I was able to post this before we sail to San Francisco for our orders. It makes me smile to picture you following my journeys on the globe. We have been greeted with open arms everywhere we go. The Brazilian Navy was in full force when we entered the harbor of Rio, known as the most beautiful one in the world. I am fortunate to be the assistant navigator, which permits me to be on the bridge entering and leaving port, so I get a firsthand view of anything of interest, and the harbor of Rio was a magnificent sight.

It was a torturous passage through the Strait of Magellan with all sorts of mayhem due to the South Pole, but under the command of Adm. Evans, we fought the fog and the currents, and cheered when we reached the open Pacific. Now I am in San Diego, enjoying the great hospitality of a beautiful American city. It is warm here every day after the mist clears in the morning.

It is spring in New York and I try to place you there, but my thoughts still drift to a moonlight night. I wish I had more memories of you, perhaps laughing in the sunshine. Your letters always bring a smile to my face. Please keep writing.

Affectionately
Christian

April 17, 1908

Dear Christian,

Today, when the post came my box was filled with the salty scent of soggy letters, just as you predicted. My cozy room at Rose Hall is filled with the sights and sounds of your journey, and I am awe struck by the wonder of it. Here in New York there are signs of Spring in the air. The kids be playing a thing called stoop ball which is a new one to me, but every day I find something amazing to behold, like a great big hole in the ground for another building to rise high in the sky. I think they are calling it Bloomingdales and I believe the Commander is of his acquaintance.

School will be ending soon but I won't be taking the sea air in Newport this summer. I will miss seeing my family and friends. But now I am a New Yorker by way of Ballygar. I landed here, I study here and now I will be working here, tutoring the candidate for Barbara's scholarship. She is a lovely Italian girl from a place called Florence. How grand to have a city named for a woman, but it is said the Italians are very romantic. This will be fine practice for my student teaching with Professor Elizabeth Loeb Von Stern. It's said she is very strict so I best be washing behind me ears. Just her name scares me.

It is true I will miss walking the gorgeous cliffs of Newport, but I too am on an island though it be built on a rock. I do enjoy the great expanse of the Hudson River leading to the sea. I can pretend I am on a grand ship traveling around the world, and I will think of you.

God Speed,
Agnes

June 10, 1908

Dear Agnes,

Now I can picture you, for you write so beautifully. You are walking by the river and the breeze is blowing your hair. The sun is bright, and you hold a hand to your eyes, scanning the water. A cruise ship pulls out of its berth and heads to the open sea, passing the Statue of Liberty. You think of the day you came to these shores, and maybe the day I left.

Since I last wrote we traveled up the coast of California, stopping at several ports, and were welcomed everywhere. It is a beautiful sight to see the high mountain peaks framing the ocean in this state at the end of our continent. We have received our orders and will be going to the Far East and return via the Suez Canal and the Mediterranean. Unless our orders change we will be heading to Hawaii, New Zealand, and Japan. Tomorrow the flotilla will pass through the Golden Gate of San Francisco on our journey across the Pacific. I fear it will be a long interval now between communications, and my dearest wish is you keep your eyes on the globe and me in your thoughts. I dearly wish you will keep writing in the hopes your missives will reach me somewhere in my travels.

I bid you fond adieu for now.

Christian

August 31, 1908

Dear Christian,

A fond adieu you say. Well, isn't that a bit of the French? I can see the pictures you paint. The flotilla heading out across the Pacific, the shore and mountains at the end of our continent. California seems as far as Tahiti to me, and when I look at the map of America I'm thinking it probably is. My summer in the city brought new adventures I could never imagine. If there is something new and daring to be discovered it can be found here. Chipper hustled me downtown to a boat that took us to a place called Coney Island, an expanse of white sand right on the Atlantic, where it seemed like thousands of people were frolicking on the beach or splashing in the sea. Along this stretch were bathhouses, clam bars, rides and games. Chipper pointed to a huge building called Lunar Park, covered in electric lights. He said we will come back one evening when the lights are ablaze. It is a wonder. Electricity for all. I am hoping to buy a bathing dress and visit again with Maureen and John, but this swimming with thousands will surely take a bit of getting used to.

By now you must have reached Hawaii. I've heard there are flowers everywhere and that the ladies wear grass skirts and do a dance called the hula. There is nothing so exotic here but my friend Ria does have a dot on her head and wears a sari, so I'm not a complete novice to other cultures and I rather like them, don't you think?

School starts in but a day or two. My student, Florence, passed her entrance exams which gives me joyful peace for I have not let Barbara down. She was surely countin' on me to pull the girl through.

Soon the trees will be turning colors and the wind will sharpen off the rivers and I'll have my nose in a book and my fingers on the globe.

God Speed,
Agnes

September 20, 1908

Dear Agnes,

I did indeed reach Hawaii. Now, I must say that yes, there are wahinis (Hawaiian girls) who perform the hula and hand out leis which are long ropes of orchids, presented with a kiss. It is an ancient tradition and one the boys of the fleet embraced with great cheer.

It is a place like no other, Agnes. We had time to do some sightseeing at Diamond Head, an active volcano, and a side trip by rail to the site of a proposed Naval Base in Pearl Harbor. Isn't that a name for the imagination? The beaches are unlike any I have ever seen for they have black sand, and palm trees full of coconuts. The Hawaiian lads tried to teach a group of us how to surf ride, and though I am a fine swimmer, trying to ride a huge wave without being pummeled was a trick I did not master. In the evening, there were beautiful concerts in the moonlight under the palm trees at the old Moana Hotel. think it would enchant you as you have me.

Luckily your letter reached me there just before we shipped out to New Zealand and Australia. The fleet will also be on maneuvers at sea and there will be little chance to communicate. I so enjoyed reading of your visit to Coney Island, a place I have never seen so. I may have been in exotic Hawaii surrounded by music, and flowers, and hula ladies, yet I would much rather hold your hand and frolic in the surf with you and all those other thousands of people, even Chipper. I fear it will be a long interlude now between communications as we head to the Far East, so

a hui hou kakou
until we meet again
Christian

October 27, 1908

Dear Christian,

You are most gallant. I do say all those orchids, hulas, and kisses sound more tantalizing then Coney Island, even with all its lights. The girls here at school are having a grand time preparing for the Halloween festivities, making up costumes with all sorts of odds and ends, and carving pumpkins. It is a bit of fun to take our minds off our mid-term exams right before Thanksgiving. Halloween is a grand time in Ireland, too, for we do have a touch of the mystic in us, descended from the Druids and all.

I am getting used to this Thanksgiving feast, and will be giving a hand to Maureen who opens her inn to half of New York, it seems. She and John have made a wonderful life for themselves here in America, and they pull me in with their good cheer. We went to the musical theater, yes we did, to see the amazin' Irish performer and composer, George M. Cohan. Oh, what a night it was. He sang and danced like a leprechaun, and we were whistling the tunes like "Yankee Doodle Dandy" as we left. I guess I am becoming more of an American every day.

Your "Great White Fleet," as they are calling it now, is the pride of our President as you bring good tidings around the world.

God Speed,
Agnes

JOURNAL 1908-1909

New York City
December 20, 1908
There are more electric lights than ever in the city now and the trees seem all dressed up for Christmas. Sparkling tree ornaments and fancy clothes fill the shop windows. Barbara and Eileen are both in town, Eileen working for Mrs. Astor and Barbara, of course, attending all the holiday galas. Barbara, in her usual gracious way, invited me to tea at the Plaza Hotel in a grand room called the Palm Court. That is all very lovely, but I felt uneasy because her mother, Loretta Farrell, the haughty one, was to be in attendance. Now it is not in me nature to impress the likes of her, but I needed to appear somewhat neat and together. I had saved a bit from my summer tutoring and headed to Bloomingdales to find something decent to put on me back. The shop girls were very helpful, and I found a pretty silk shirtwaist and tan wool jacket and skirt.

Oh my, the grandeur of the Plaza was like walkin' into the Breakers the first time. Red velvet carpets, crystal chandeliers and a pink silk circular banquet filled the lobby. I had to duck my head not to get poked in the eye from the palms surrounding the tea room. Tea was served in the most elegant china, and three-tiered silver plates held scones, tea sandwiches and pastries.

Her ladyship politely inquired as to my well-being. I said I had been to the theater to see the great musical artist George M. Cohan. She simpered, "How nice," but said she preferred the opera. Who needs the likes of her, anyhow?

When Mrs. Farrell went to the powder room Barbara pulled me aside to say her father was worried about Christian. The fleet was caught in a great typhoon in the Pacific, and she wondered if I had heard from him. Hearing that made my resolve weaken. I said it had been months since his last missive, and I thought I should move on, for surely, he was far above me in society.

Barbara said I shouldn't be thinking such thoughts, for the rest of the family were not like her mother, who she knew was a snob. She said her father's side of the family came from a tradition of service in the navy, and they are a kind, open family who found success through hard work and sacrifice.

I said surely she inherited her charm and goodness from them. She laughed. Yes, she had grown up in a naval family, and knew that long separations are stressful on wives and sweethearts. Wives and sweethearts! She's gone daft. Then her mother headed our way, smiling and greeting people, waving like the damn queen.

So, there I was, Agnes Logan, adrift in the Plaza Hotel in New York City, feeling like I was sinking into the deep black bog of home.

February 15, 1909
It is bleak and grey and cold and I am feeling just the same. Still nary a note from Christian. I have been writing little cheery notes about New York, and George M. Cohan, and tea at the Plaza, but no word. He is a man of the world, a proper gentleman, with adventures beyond my wildest dreams. I'm thinking his courtin' idea was a whim of the moment for a seaman leaving on a long voyage. As his letters travel around the globe, I am here in my simple life, though a breathless moment in time will always linger in my heart. How is it possible that so much time has passed and yet I can still feel the power of the moment we met.

It is at times like these that I miss my Fey, my dearest friend so far away. I wrote her about Christian and she answered I must not doubt myself, for I am indeed a strong womanly force. Tis true I have some brains in me head and a bit of wit, but maybe there's something in me I just can't see. She was always the flirty one and caught her man with a flutter of her lashes. I worry a bit, though, for she seems a bit pinched in her letters, feeling the pressure of over two years married and no baby. I 'm wondering about that.

I never told Maureen about Christian for she would be actin' all romantic and asking me questions I can't answer. As it is she fusses I will be a nun without some fun in me life. She may be right.

Time to put some roses back in me cheeks, I'm thinkin.

March 12, 1909

This indeed was a day of great excitement and a bit of danger, I'd say. My professor of history, Mary Willard, has been talking us up about the Women's Suffrage Movement. She arranged for us to go to the rally and parade today. Me and my buddies, Ria and Sun Yi, walked over to 57th Street to watch, and Eileen joined us from Mrs. Astor's. It was an inspiring event to see. Hundreds of women dressed in white were carrying flags and banners demanding the right to vote. Of course, I cheered them on, though not bein' a citizen I can't vote.

As we were waving and clapping, a couple of shaggy lookin' hooligans started heckling us. They were yelling, "Go back where yer came from," pointing and laughing at Ria and Sun Yi. "Hey look, a dot and a chink," they yelled to the crowd. Then when they noticed Eileen's flaming red hair they started calling us Micks. I stood my ground in front of them, I did. I said to leave us alone and one of them spit on the sidewalk and grabbed me arm. So I kicked him right in the shin. He was madder than Mrs. O'Flarity when some rascals took her cow, he was. He grabbed for me and I swung my duffle at him.

Then, in a flash, a blur of dark blue stepped in, grabbed the troublemakers and handcuffed them. Before he led them to the paddy wagon he looked back and said, "Wait here, ladies." Me friends were in tears, but Eileen and I stood proud, protecting them. We huddled near the side of a building, and the nosy crowd went on their way.

As he strode back to us, I thought he was a fine specimen of Irish manhood, I'd say. Eileen poked me in the ribs and fanned herself. Oh, I knew he was Irish. He was a policeman, and he had those dark almost black Irish eyes that held a gleam, even though this was a serious situation. He tipped his hat, and said, "Officer Francis Molloy at your service." He asked for our names and if were injured in any way. Ria and Sun Yi were very shy, due to the trauma I am sure. Eileen looked him straight in the eye and said, "Eileen Burns, and this is my friend Agnes Logan." He smiled. He had a dimple. Then he said, "And aren't you two lasses a sight to behold. I'll be needing your information for my report."

Oh, the blarney, I'm thinking. He said he would escort us, for the city was a bit on edge today and we needed to be careful. All the way people greeted him like he was the mayor or someone. He was sharing a smile and a joke with the vendors and shopkeepers on 57th Street. For sure he was a bit of a show off, no matter how good looking he thinks he is. Eileen was buyin' his charm like a box of crackerjacks, and he kept glancing at her and took her arm. When we got to the Astor's he knew the doorman, of course. He said he was delivering one Eileen Burns who was beset upon by troublemakers, then he tipped his hat to her and said he'd be seein' her again. Something is definitely brewing there.

April 5, 1909
I need to take a big deep breath. My studies are doing well and another year has passed, but I'm believing I need to have some fun. Now, I'm not complaining, but it's been school, studyin', work, and change. So much change since I first landed on these shores three years ago. Just adapting from one year to the next has challenged me best nature. Soon I will begin tutoring Barbara's new prospect. I have met her. She is an American girl, very bright, with that get up and go attitude of a New Yorker. Nothing daunts her. I think I will have my hands full with this one.

So, I took a bit of a break and went downtown to see Maureen and John. They've been in a bit of turmoil expanding their place. Maureen said it was fate that the building next door went up for sale. John knew the realtor and the Commander put in a good word. She said the hammerin' and bangin' are slowing down business but once it is done, she will have room for a baby. Won't it be a marvel for them to have a little one.

When I got there John came in for lunch and we were chatting up. I told them my story of Officer Molloy and his rescue of us girls. John slapped his big hand on the table and said, "Would that be Francis Molloy?" John says he knows Francis and his Pa, who owns Pete's Tavern near Gramercy Park. He says it's a fine place and that O'Henry wrote the "Gift of the Magi" there. It's a good thing I had some learning about short stories in my literature class, for I heard of him and nodded in my most intelligent manner.

Maureen sat there grinning and stirring her tea. So, John goes on about how George runs the bar, Peter runs the restaurant, Joseph is a city councilman and Francis a cop. It seems that Mrs. Molloy is the smiling face and hostess of it all. I told them I thought

Francis was sweet on Eileen. Maureen huffed a bit and said he was a good catch, so I best keep that in mind. Then John looked over at me and raised his bushy Irish brows at me and tilted his head toward Maureen. He knew! He knew about Christian, no doubt form having a pint with the Commander. What a rascal. And so, my secret was out. Maureen was miffed, and said she hoped I wasn't wasting my youth on a mystery man across the world when such a fine specimen as Francis Molloy was in my sights. I laughed then and said I think Francis may have met his match in Eileen. Then she opened a cabinet, took out some whiskey, offered a toast and said, "Things they are lookin' up!"

Maybe they are. I still keep me eye on the globe.

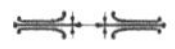

May 10, 1909

Spring has blown in like happy daffodils. I keep my spirits high for an abandoned letter writer and keep my own counsel, for I need no talk from Barbara of that sweetheart nonsense. Barbara is too romantic, for she went off and married that count under the influence of her social climbing mom, Loretta. My feelin' is that Aunt Loretta has a debutante all picked out for Christian when his feet hit solid land again and he will be done with the likes of me. Spirits high, now girl.

There have been many glad tidings from home. Charlie is graduating as an electrical engineer of all things and will be using his new-found skills on a great ship being built in Belfast. He says he is part of a team of 15,000 workmen of all types; carpenters, cabinet makers, painters and electricians. I can't even imagine such a thing. We are all so proud of him, little Charlie, who has made a grand success of his chance to become something. Father Shea is so puffed up he's now recruiting other lads to follow in Charlie's footsteps.

Mum says the winter was a mild one so the cottage, fences and barn need just a bit of work, which is a boon to the boys who share the burden of all the chores, along with Pa. She wrote she gives an earful to Mrs. O'Hara about my adventures in this great America. I can picture such a scene with Mum saying I went for tea at the fanciest hotel in New York, of all things. It is good for me to keep me sense of humor, for there is a sadness that comes upon me when the grass is green and the birds be chirpin' and I be thinkin' of my meadow by the brook.

No word from Fey, and I worry about her, for she is such a free spirit and James has a high opinion of himself.

At school, we are all working like crazy rabbits trying to keep our grades and get ready for our graduation. We are to wear long white dresses with satin bows and a sprig of forget-me-knots in our hair. Sun Li's mother has a tailor at the laundry who is sewing our gowns. She says he is in her debt and I don't doubt it, for she is a taskmaster at best. He speaks no English, so when we show up for our fittings he points and nods and we twirl around, giggling like school girls. But, then, we are, aren't we?

Time for my books. Maybe tomorrow I'll check the globe again, for I can be a foolish girl.

June 21, 1909

Today was the grandest day, my graduation! Our class gathered in the great hall with our friends and family looking on, and Thomas Hunter himself handed me my diploma. Maura and John and Chipper were there, my friend Eileen, and Barbara and the Commander. Sure, as I predicted way back, he and John have become friends, and they sat together beaming like two proud fathers. Oh, how I wish my Mum and Pa could have been here to see me and I them. It was a bittersweet moment. I will soon have a picture of our lovely graduating class, bright in our white dresses, our smiles of thanks for the gift of this wonderful free education and a promise for the future.

After the ceremony, Commander Farrell took us to the New York Athletic Club for dinner. We were a bit awed at first by the privileged setting. The dark wood paneled walls, soft sconces, and immaculate staff at our disposal found us speaking in low tones. Once dinner began the Commander made a toast to "Our very special Agnes Logan, the first recipient of the Barbara Farrell Scholarship whose wit, brains, and charm never faltered." Well then, everyone raised a glass and applauded, even the wait staff who were lingering on the side. It is not like me to be easily overwhelmed, but at that moment I was and I felt a tear touch me cheek. Then I offered a toast to Barbara whose kindness and vision will open many doors to young ladies who want to improve their lives. The champagne kept flowing, and the toasts kept coming and the wait staff kept clapping. Oh, what a night!!

Thank you, thank you, thank you Mary, God, St. Agnes, Mum, Pa, me brothers Pat and Mike and Charlie, my dear friend Fey for giving me hope. May you all keep me safe in your hearts.

June 23, 1909

My thoughts are running in circles today as I clean out my room at Rose Hall. How can it be that my time here is over? It seems just a moment ago, I tremulously climbed the steps to Hunter College so terrified I thought I'd freeze in place. Now I am a certified teacher and will begin at the elementary school in the fall and tutor the new scholarship candidate this summer.

Maureen and John saved a room for me in the new expanded inn, and I can take the subway uptown from City Hall. I feel like a genuine New Yorker, thanks to Chipper. The stations are very nice and clean, with lovely tile pictures at every stop for those who do not read well. Well, there is a fish at Fulton Street and a beaver at Astor Place. They are very clever here, I'm thinking.

Norah and Tom have given me a graduation present and asked me to spend some time with them in Newport before my tutoring begins. I feel like one of the fancies heading to me summer home. The best is I will be traveling with Eileen on the boat where we first met, and that will be great fun for us both. She is all mooning over Francis Molloy now that she's leaving New York for the summer. He is a bit of a rascal, that one, so I do worry he'll be out and about after he waves goodbye, though he does seem smitten by the beautiful Eileen. Listen to myself, going on about them two, for I am certainly not a winner in the romance department of life. Now Newport beckons and I will surely be thinking of Christian. I know from Prof. Higgins the fleet passed through the Suez Cannel on the last leg of its journey. My emotions are in a dither, relieved for his safe passage and distressed I have had not a word.

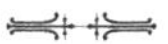

June 25, 1909
A letter came today as I was packing to leave. I can barely breathe.

April 1909

Dear Agnes,

By now you must think I have fallen into the Pacific Ocean and am lost at sea, and there are moments when it has seemed so. I wrote to you from Australia and Japan and Egypt where we went ashore, but I think it might be a miracle if you every received them. I am proud to have served in such an endeavor that will one day be in the history books, but it has taken its toll on my sense of time and place.

Agnes, I have met a king, King George of Denmark, seen a leper colony in Molakai, Hawaii, watched a native Maori dance in New Zealand, rode a camel in Egypt and even saw the Great Sphinx in the moonlight. But it was not the Newport moonlight on the night we met, and I keep that perfect picture of you close to my heart.

We are now in Gibraltar, the last leg of our journey, and mail awaited us there. I was overjoyed when I found your letters, to know you have not yet deserted me. Each one is a jewel that brings me near to where you are: the Palm Court at the Plaza Hotel, the Suffragettes march, your night at the theater or simply following the fleet with your hand on the globe.

Soon we will be setting sail for the Suez Canal, and even when we arrive home I will have duties to fulfill before my leave, and then I will find you, I will.

With much affection,
Christian

I read it over and over again until the paper was getting worn. He will find me, he said. Now that will take some doing as I am heading to Newport with Eileen, and no telling where in the world he is now. Can I still believe in miracles?

June 30, 1909
I can barely put words to it. Norah and Tom and the boys met us at the boat and we all gleefully piled into their carriage for our ride

down Thames Street. Eileen went to the Beechwood Estate to prepare for Mrs. Astor and I settled into my cozy attic room. I rested a bit, but the memories of Christian kept intruding, so to make myself even more miserable, I walked to the cliffs.

The afternoon sun felt warm and healing as I looked out at the ocean crashing against the rocks. I strolled a bit and found a bench where I sat inhaling the scents of salt and seaweed, and I just breathed it in, trying to clear me head. A motion caught my eye, and when I turned a tall figure in dazzling white was striding purposely toward me. I put my hand to my eyes to shield the sun for surely I was seeing things. Then the figure called my name, and I knew. I gathered my skirt and ran straight toward him as if my legs weren't my own. And then his arms were around me, "I found you, my beautiful Agnes Logan," he whispered. He gently held me at arm's length and we stared at each other. His eyes sparkled like blues sapphires in the sun. He put his head back and laughed and said he'd imagined me in the daylight, even to the freckles on my nose. Even then I thought I must be in a daydream and would waken any moment. He touched his hand to my cheek, drew me into him and our lips met, and once again the world shifted on its axis.

July 4, 1909

My thoughts are still a bit in a scramble. I've been dutifully trying to keep my journal, scribbly as it is. Seems Christian caused quite a stir up here at Norah's. She said when he appeared in his smart whites the boys were all agog at the sight of this impressive stranger. Even Norah, who has her proper ways, was so taken with him and his story that she felt it acceptable to send him along to me. He is studying at the Naval War College in Newport and was about to head off to New York when Barbara told him I was here. Seems fate keeps throwing us together on the cliffs that look toward Ireland. It be a good omen I think.

When we got back, Norah took me aside and said I'd been holding out on her. I told her no one but Barbara and my friend Fey in Ireland knew we'd been corresponding, and I had no intentions of pretending it was anything more.

But it is much more. Tom got out the Jamison's and he and Christian went into his study. They came out all smilin' and Christian walked me out to the porch, took my hand and asked if he could court me. In my most demure way, which is hard for me for I rather tramp through, life I said, "Lieutenant, you know I've never been courted, for I must have been waitin' for you."

I have to write Fey I'm learning how to flirt!

August 15, 1909

God Bless Maureen and John. I have a quiet place with a sitting area and my own bathroom. Can hardly believe it. The inn is busier than ever since the expansion. Chipper is a young gentleman now, almost twenty years old, can you believe it? He set up a tourist business in the inn and keeps running the guests all over town, a feat he does so well. In a few weeks, I will begin teaching at the elementary school connected with Hunter College. I have the syllabus and all my pencils sharpened. Mrs. Von Stern will supervise me in the beginning which I am grateful for. The thought of facing twenty little faces of all shapes and colors has me nerves a bit in a jangle, but I'm ready, yes I am.

Christian comes to visit when he can and has charmed them all. Maureen said he was a fine specimen and surely smitten.

Eileen managed to get out of the grip of Mrs. Astor for a few days, much to the delight of one Francis Molloy and we all went to

Coney Island. Chipper led the way like the good tourist guide he is. It was the grandest of days. We stayed till the lights came on in Luna Park, blazing so bright they hid the light of the moon.

⸻

September 20, 1909

Today Liam McGilligutty put gum in Mary Ellen's long blond hair. My first crisis!! She was screamin' bloody murder, so loudly Mrs. Chauncey came in to see what the commotion was all about. I sent Liam to sit in the corner and firmly told him not to move an inch. Then Mrs. Von Stern took Mary Ellen to the kitchen to put some olive oil on her hair to remove the gum.

The class was holding themselves to keep from giggling, but I managed to settle them down. I told them if they behaved I'd tell them a story about Ireland. Oh, do they love my stories about riding my horse and looking for the Tinkers. Liam says I sound like his Nana, who I think came over during the potato famine. It's a miracle she made it, for those ships were not fit for a beast, much less the destitute Irish souls on board. They are grand kids, but I'm thinking I might like to be a counselor, like Mrs. Von Stern. More studying for that, but maybe I could do a course or two while I'm teaching. I do so enjoy the tutoring of Barbara's girls, the feeling that I'm giving something back of all that I have learned in my journey. I met with Dean Wadleigh. She was supportive but also cautious as to the amount of work it required especially with my teaching responsibilities. It may take me two years instead of one but I've set my mind to it.

I have to keep my head straight. Christian has two years of school and training for his master's degree in strategic studies, and then he will be a Lt. Col. I wonder if I can be a part of such a life, or if our future is even in his thoughts. He keeps me off balance and flushed by his amazin' presence but my doubts bubble up like a cold spring in the woods.

November 20, 1909

Today was our last day before that great American Thanksgiving holiday. The children were so excited. They made orange paper turkeys that I pinned on their coats to bring home to their ma and pa. I made sure they were all bundled up, for the air is crisp. I checked Mary Ellen's long blond hair, just in case. Liam, always incorrigible, said his ma was making a goose, so nothing would do but a goose cutout. They marched out and I waved goodbye. I put on my wool jacket and tam for my walk to the downtown subway and the warmth of my cozy room at Maureen's.

I was happy, strolling along absorbed in my thoughts. Distracted, it took me a moment to register who was standing there before me. He had a quizzical smile, and a tilt to his head, and said, "Am I beholding the beautiful Agnes Logan, or has she forgotten me?" He was holding some licorice sticks and a bouquet of flowers. I took a step back to appraise him. Then I laughed and said he was surprising me again, but please pass the licorice. Our hands met and we melded like music in the brisk November air.

November 23, 1909

What a grand weekend! We 'd sit in Maureen's kitchen and laugh and tell stories, then off we would go for an adventure in the city. Chipper took us to Times Square for lunch at Child's, which is an automat. Well, I've never seen such a place. One puts a nickel in a slot and out pops a pie! On Saturday night, we went to the Arcadia ballroom with Eileen, Frances, and Chipper, with a lovely girl on his arm and we danced the night away. When Christian took me in his arms, we were transported back to the moment our eyes met across the ballroom at The Breakers, and he whispered, "I will never forget the night I found you."

After Mass on Sunday we sat in the parlor. He said it was time I met his family and asked me to go home with him for Thanksgiving. Oh, dear Lord. Every fear and hurdle I'd met since I stepped off that boat from Ireland washed over me like a giant wave from the great Atlantic. He must have seen the color leave my cheeks for he knelt before me with great concern and asked if I was all right. I told him I wasn't at all prepared for such a journey, for we were just finding our way with each other. He treats me like the queen of the realm and thinks everyone else will too, but I truly have my doubts. I am a poor Irish immigrant blessed with some brains and ambition but I am fearful. 'Tis true Barbara and the Commander have embraced me but there is a sniff of snobbery in the atmosphere when haughty Loretta is present. He gently pushed a stray curl off my cheek and led me to the large mirror over the console table. He said, "Look, Agnes, look at us." And I saw. I saw us. A handsome man and a lovely woman matched in a magnetic pull, Agnes and Christian, as it should be.

December 5, 1909
Prof. Chauncy would be tweaking my ears if she knew I've been so remiss with my journaling, but how can one write when caught in a typhoon, and that I was. And so, I went with Christian to Boston. I had but a day to prepare and Maura scooted me to Macy's to get

some proper clothes. I do look fine at my teaching job in simple dark skirts and jackets, and some pretty blouses to add a bit of color. We found a lovely day dress in a deep burgundy and a soft grey woolen cape and a new pair of fancy shoes. She said my suits were fine for the journey. The journey. Oh my.

Christian, always the proper gentleman, arranged for a friend of his who was also going home to Boston to travel with us. He works at the New York Stock Exchange. Though it is just around the corner from Maureen's, it is a world unto itself and way beyond my comprehension. He was charming, this Wesley Myers, tall and fair and rich, but not full of himself at all. By the end of our journey I was ready for some match-making for Barbara.

Christian's brother, Luke, met us with the car and was so easy-going I forgot to be nervous. That, and him being the spitting image of Christian put me at ease. We pulled up to a brownstone not far from Barbara's. It truly seemed welcoming with pots of bright fall flowers leading up to the door. Christian took my hand and in we went.

The parlor was grand but comfortable and smelled of cinnamon. Christian called out we had arrived. A lovely slim woman with an apron wrapped around her hurried into the room and grabbed him in a big hug. When he stepped back, he grabbed my hand. "Mom, this is Agnes, Agnes Logan." I did a little curtsy. She held out her arms, and with smiling her blue eyes, said, "Agnes, you are so welcome, and I want you to call me Patsy."

Just then I saw the Commander coming down the stairs. To add to my discomfort at being the center of attention, now I was confused. He came toward me, took my hands in his big strong mitts and said, "Captain Eugene Farrell at your service. My twin brother Frank holds you in high esteem." I must have looked like a goldfish in a bowl with my mouth agape. The door flew open and in came the real Commander and Barbara, all happy and full of themselves. And then I laughed for this was truly a joke on me. Before I could recover a teenage girl all out of breath rushed in. "I'm Lucy, Christian's sister, and I've been just dying to meet you!" She grabbed my hand and said she just loved romance and I should come to her room for she wanted to know everything. Christian said to mind her manners and she scooted off in a huff. Then we all sat down for a glass of sherry and a holiday toast. Dear St. Mary, I must confess I sure needed a bit of the spirits to get me breathin' again.

Barbara was all flushed and beautiful, gaily laughing with her cousins. When the bell rang, she ran to answer it. It was Wesley, all spit and polish and tall and handsome. The two of them just stood there staring at each other like statues. I knew it. Christian caught my eye and winked. The devil I say! He knew too.

Sure enough, Loretta arrived with her haughty head high and took a long approving look at Wesley, practically drooling at the possibilities. Good thing, too, for I escaped her superior attitude. Instead of being so uppity, she should have some remorse for foisting that slimy count on her lovely girl.

Wesley escorted me back to New York. We were a pair, alright. Me still dreaming of Christian's goodbye kiss and the warm embrace of his family, and him mooning over Barbara. He'll be seeing her when she comes to New York next month and he asked me how we manage being apart so much. I said I really wasn't sure, but we both have very busy lives and that eases the strain. As the train rumbled through Connecticut I drifted off into a magical world where dreams come true.

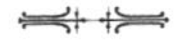

January 20, 1910
T'was the end of another long week of teaching the wee ones and rushing off to psychology and statistics classes for my degree. It's been cold and dreary so my thinking was I'd cheer up the children with a story for they do so love my Irish tales. I gathered them all around me and though they were itching for the bell to ring, I put my finger to my lips and they settled in, eyes wide.

So, there I be, telling them about the day Fey and I met a leprauchan carrying a bag of gold. He had a long white beard and was wearing a red weskit and shoes that curled up at the toes. When we chanced upon him he was so mad he shook his shillelagh at us and said he would put an evil spell on us. Fey flounced her flaming red hair and laughed, which only made him madder and madder. Our horses began prancin' and whinnying and he backed off a bit. Then I asked him if he would like to feed the horses. He squinted up his eyes and said we were trickin' him. Fey handed him an apple and Blackie bowed down and smiled at him and batted his big long horse lashes. Then he laughed the strangest leprechaun laugh, bowed and said to he had to get going before he got all riled up again.

Just as I was finishing the tale I heard a soft chuckle from the doorway. It was the great Thomas Hunter himself. "Good afternoon, Miss Logan, I've been enjoying your story," he said. I managed to straighten myself out just as the bell rang and the children lined up neatly and left. I was disheveled and flustered, but I curtsied. "Please," he said and gestured for me to sit at my desk, which I was very grateful to do.

He said he heard I was taking my degree courses and thought I would become an excellent counselor. My first student, Florence, was doing very well, now in her second year, and my young upstart New Yorker was a handful but holding her own. "I want to speak to you about the Foundation."

He felt there were young women in New York who could benefit from the scholarship, but that we needed to spread the word. It seems that a colleague of his, a philanthropist named Jacob Sciff, had provided buildings for the charity, The Henry Street Settlement. Founded by Lillian Wald, a humanitarian, it offers many services to the poor including health care, social and recreational programs. He asked me to be an advocate and speaker for the Foundation for Hunter College by telling my story and encouraging young women to better themselves.

"We'll start there, and set up a schedule for other organizations who work with the poor."

Well, I never. This was not the time to be flummoxed if he wanted me to go out speaking. I said I was honored to carry the message, and I did have a lively tale to tell. He crinkled his eyes in a smile and said, "My dear, you have always been one of our very special young ladies." Now I could be getting all puffed up, but will try to remain my modest self, Agnes Logan, the lecturer!

March 17, 1910
T'was a great day for the Irish! Me, Eileen, Chipper and John and Maureen all gathered for the St. Patrick's Day parade up Fifth Avenue. We were wearing green berets and waved our Irish flags as the marching bands and dignitaries strode past. Thomas Hunter had the honor of being the Grand Marshall and closed the school for the day. What a treat!

We were keeping our eyes open for Francis Molloy who was marching with the New York City Police Department. When his contingent came by we all hooted and hollered but he stayed in step, his eyes straight ahead. After the parade, we gathered at Pete's Tavern where lots of beer, music and laughter abounded.

In the midst of all this revelry Francis jumped up on the bar and called for attention. The crowd started shouting, "Francis, Francis, Francis!" He laughed and told us to pipe down. Eileen said, "Has he gone daft?" Then he said that a year ago at another parade he met the beautiful Eileen Burns and he'd been courting her ever since. Then he knelt down, took her hand and asked her to marry him!!

The place erupted. "Say yes, say yes," they all shouted. Eileen with a twinkle in her eye said, "If I be sayin' yes in front of all these witnesses, I guess I can't back out." Then Francis hoisted her up on the bar and said, "Drinks on the house!"

We're all still recovering.

ONE YEAR LATER

Spring 1911

Mrs. Patrick Logan
Ros Leana Farm
Ballygar, County Galway
Ireland

May 1, 1911

Dear Mum,

Our joy is spilling out all over the streets of New York. Maureen and John have two babies, twins they are, a boy and a girl, George and Juliet. George for strength and Juliet for love; now isn't that a delight. Norah and Tom made the trip to New York for their Christening, as did Commander Farrell since he and John are as close as two sailors on a raft at sea. Norah was here, her usual prim and proper self, and rather terrified to go traipsing around New York with Chipper. For sure she saw more then she bargained for, I'd say, especially when he took her to Chinatown. Can you imagine? 'Tis true New York can be a bit overwhelming with such a hodgepodge all thrown together.

Norah's boys were full of the adventure at all the sights and sounds and wonders and they followed Chipper around like a puppy dogs. They saw the Statue of Liberty, they did, and the Brooklyn Bridge and those brave boys even ventured into the subway. When we took the electric trolley up the great Broadway, my thoughts flew back with awe to my first adventure here when I was but two days off the boat.

Now I am a professional woman with initials after my name, can you believe? I do so savor my work with the college and the foundation. With me busy in New York and Christian in Newport or places unknown it is a darn good thing I'm not sitting around crocheting doilies waiting for a knock on the door.

Mum, the white lace curtains are billowing in the breeze on this soft May evening, and the sounds of the city are dimmed in my cozy room. I could be daydreaming of home, but babies are crying so I'm heading downstairs to give Maureen an extra hand. Love to Pa and the boys.

Your loving daughter,
Agnes

Miss Agnes Logan
c/o Galvin's Emerald Inn
10 Maiden Lane
New York, New York

May 5, 1911

Dear Agnes,

It was so lovely to see you at the babies' Christening. The inn is quite delightful and we were so pleased to have such a meaningful visit with the family. That Chipper fellow took us around the city, but all that razzle dazzle is not for me. I don't know how you can even get on that underground train. Then again, you surprise me at every turn.

Christian was here for Sunday dinner and he brought sailor hats for the boys. We are his adopted Newport family and he feels right at home here. The boys were all over him, wanting to hear more of his stories of his travels around the world. He said he was hoping you could come for a visit over the fourth after school is out, and of course you're more than welcome here. I hope to hear from you soon.

Norah

Lt. Christian Farrell
Newport War College
Residence 10
Cushing Road
Newport, Rhode Island

May 12, 1911

My Dear Christian,

Maybe I'm missing a letter from you for its a bit confusing sometimes to keep up with your comings and goings, and I do have obligations here with the new babies and the young ladies for the scholarship. I fear the fates are fooling us, for the stars are not aligned for me to visit Newport in July. I am a working woman after all and have commitments to the foundation and the college. The school has provided me an office and I do get some breezes from the East River, but the heat of the summer has yet to arrive. For sure, I will be missing Newport on the hot, humid days and I treasure every moment I was blessed to be in its soft embrace.

In a way, it is a fine thing that my life is a busy one, for it eases the absence of you. I just have to hold tighter to the sweet memories of our every encounter.

Affectionately,
Agnes

Miss Agnes Logan
c/o Galvin's Emerald Inn
10 Maiden Lane
New York, New York

May 20, 1911

My Dear Agnes,

I have been suitably chastised. Is this our first disagreement? I fear Norah spoke out of turn for I was awaiting my orders to see if I would be free over the Fourth of July holiday before I ventured to ask you to make the journey here. I will have leave until July 15th when I go to sea for four months to complete my degree in Strategic Studies.

My darling Agnes, you constantly amaze me with all you do, and how your brilliance shames the bright lights of the city. I would never presume, and yet I ache to see you where we first met, for Newport is now in my heart as are you. Please take my loving thoughts and reconsider making the journey here.

Please, bear with me just a little longer. Always remember, wherever the wind blows I will find you.

Lovingly,
Christian

Lt. Christian Farrell
Newport War College
Residence 10
Cushing Road
Newport, Rhode Island

June 1, 1911

Dear Christian,

'Tis true I was a bit miffed, more at Norah I think, for she can be a bossy one. Now I am once again touched by your lovely words of persuasion. Yet I feel we are both at a crossroads as we each have reached our long-sought goals, your master's degree and my baccalaureate. My parchment hangs on the office wall and each day I look at it with wonder.

I feel settled and productive, and believe I have found my footing at last. My longing to see you has been a constant for all this time. It is true that I miss you, but that seems to be the way our path has unfolded, a moment in time and then months to remember that moment. You asked that I bear with you, and I ask the same, as my journey unfolds here in the city. Perhaps we are like ships that pass in the night, each reaching but never to be together, as you fly across the seas and I stride the city streets, my feet securely planted on Lexington Avenue.

Affectionately,
Agnes

Miss Agnes Logan
c/o Galvin's Emerald Inn
10 Maiden Lane
New York, New York

June 15, 1911

Dear Agnes,

Christian came home for a short visit before his next mission which will be take him to sea for four months, at least. He is bereft for he fears you may be pulling away from him and was dashed when you rather firmly refused to come to Newport.

Your commitment to the foundation is more than admirable, and your mission with Thomas Hunter to enlighten and encourage disadvantaged young women is of untold value. But, my dear friend and colleague, it was never my intention that you should feel unable to take a short holiday. I confess I have been rather careless these past months, putting the burden on your fine shoulders. I have been in a maelstrom of activity preparing for my wedding to Wesley. Need I say that mother is in high spirits overseeing this extravaganza she has planned, just as she did with my ill-fated marriage to the count. I think Daddy, Wesley and I need to take her in hand as we feel a simpler, more sedate event is appropriate.

We will be visiting Newport over the fourth, not to attend any fancy balls, but spend some time with friends of father at the New York Yacht Club. He will be in New York at the end of June for a regatta at the club and would be more then delighted to have you sail to Newport with him and Wesley who is coming for the weekend. We will arrange for passage back on the Fall River Line. I would dearly wish to see you for your counsel as you have always been impervious to my mother's high-handed machinations.

Please telephone me next Sunday at noon and reverse the charges for a long-distance call. My number is Beacon Hill 2-3298. Awaiting your decision.

As always,
Barbara

Mrs. James O'Connell
21 Ballygar Road
Ballygar, County Galway
Ireland

June 17, 1911

Dearest Fey,

Oh, how I miss you, for I wish I were with you under the Rose of Sharon tree. Leave it to me to be caught up in the strangest romance. The last I saw Christian was in April over the Easter Holiday. We strolled along Fifth Avenue. Flowers and finery filled the avenue, the ladies in the highest style of fashion. I felt a bit out of place in my simple frock coat and straw bonnet, but Christian bought me violets and tucked them into the blue velvet band. And each time he leaves I wonder how will it be when we meet again? I fear I am losing faith in us.

As you know, I set my cocky head on being a counselor and received my bachelor's degree just last week. Fey, I have learned to use the meager gifts bestowed on me and hone them, trust them, keep moving forward and keep my fears tucked beneath my bloomers, certainly a place no one can see.

I feel you are hiding your fears, too. You are surely suffering, wondering if there will be a child one day. If I were there we'd be making faces at the old hags and sneaking frogs into their baskets. You are strong, beautiful and bright so hold that flaming head high.

I have found that the gift of work is a great leveler to face the day with confidence. So it is grand that you're a partner in the business and expanding the pharmacy. Your smartness with that accounting business will be making you a wealthy one someday, and then you and James can sail across the sea.

So much, so much in such a few short years it seems. My love always and write when the moment comes.

Your loving friend,
Agnes

Miss Agnes Logan
c/o Galvin's Emerald Inn
10 Maiden Lane
New York, New York
USA

June 21, 1911

My Darlin' Agnes,

I lit a candle for those two little wee ones and thanked the Lord for the kindness of the Galvin family. How lovely they are to have kept you close in their warm embrace. Now that you be safe in me prayers I have news that has sent me and Pa and the whole of Ballygar in a tither like no other. You'll be needin' to hold yer breath now, my sweet girl. I have gone and won the Irish Sweepstakes! I have. Now, it's not a fortune for they don't pick just one ticket, but enough pounds to be puttin' away fer a rainy day and maybe a wee taste of high livin', not that Pa has a mind for such things.

We had a grand celebration at the pub and Pat and Mike bought Guinness for everyone. Now I'm thinkin' my purse strings need to be tucked away. So, I'll be biden' me time, for now, me winnings safe in the bank gainin' interest for the day I can come to the great New York on that ship Charlie is building. I did get me a wool jumper and some sturdy leather boots with a bit of the fashion for Mass on Sunday.

Father Shea is leadin' a group of us up to Tara Hill for the summer solstice celebration, and we'll be lightin' a bonfire in honor of St. John the Baptist in the Christian manor. Druids will be there too in their long black robes and staffs doin' their mumbo jumbo. The longest day it is, now the sun will be settin' after ten and our spirits will open in the long summer days.

You are always in our thoughts, burstin' with pride for our lovely girl so far away.

Your loving mum.
Rose

Miss Agnes Logan
c/o Galvin's Emerald Inn
10 Maiden Lane
New York, New York
USA

June 25, 1911

My dearest friend Agnes,

I, too, wish you were here under the Rose of Sharon, a place where our cares were simple ones. You have been delicate and kept your counsel about my situation, but there are days when the burden of being barren overwhelms me. I do keep me back straight but seem to be spendin' more time with Blackie than James. As each month passes it creates more strain on our marriage so instead of sittin' and stewin', we are aiming to solve this dilemma. We went to a specialist in infertility problems in Dublin and he was not encouraging as it seems I have some blockage in my tubes. He told us about a doctor in New York at the University Medical Center who has a procedure to correct this condition, the very latest in medical science.

Now, Agnes, don't be jumping up and down yet, for we are saving up to make the trip, and it may be another year. You are so right, my smart friend, my work is a great leveler and now we are earning more as the business expands so this is possible.

And again, congratulations to you for your degree in counseling. You are a wonder and a pride to all Irish womanhood. I can't imagine such a long-distance romance as you and Christian, but you have weathered long separations and always find your way back to each other. Keep the faith, me brave Agnes.

Your loving friend,
Fey

JOURNAL 1911-1912

New York City
June 30, 1911
What a to do about me getting to Newport. You'd think I was some bloody aristocrat instead of a hard-working woman respecting my responsibilities. I would be lying to myself if I wasn't flattered by all this dam attention, and yet I feel I've been swept forward in the wind, finding ground, then lifted again through days of wonder and fear and joy.

It seems I created quite a stir when I wrote that my feet were firmly planted on Lexington Avenue. I wasn't trying to be difficult, but all this coming and going these past few years has left a strain on my emotions. I needed to get a grip on myself and not fall into the enchantment of being with Christian for a few short days and then the cycle of separation. I am not sure I can continue on this conflicted path of high and low emotions.

But now I am committed to the journey for I would be a very foolish woman to refuse Barbara's generous offer. I asked for a few more days over the holiday which will not be a problem, but I believe it is less about me then my connection to the Farrell Foundation. Maureen said I should stop at Bloomingdales tomorrow and get a new summer frock. Who knows, I may even find a yachting outfit. Now don't I sound just grand!

Newport, RI
July 4, 1911
I am hardly able to put words to it for today, July 4, 1911, Christian proposed to me, Agnes Logan, former lady's maid, thank you very much!

When I made my way over to the East River to meet the Commander, he swooped me into the Norah B. and we sailed up the river to Long Island Sound and the open sea. When the cliffs of Newport came into view the memories of my first journey here flooded my heart.

Barbara gaily waved from the yacht club when we arrived and said that Christian would pick me up at Norah's that evening. I was truly happy to see Norah and Tom and the boys all full of questions and excited that their hero was coming. I was on the porch taking a breeze and the aroma of the honeysuckle when I saw him striding up the street. He waved to George Shea who was having his evening libation and nosing around as usual. My heart did triple turns as it does when I see him, this brilliant handsome man who somehow cares for me and for sure my heart was in peril.

That night we strolled to the cliffs remembering how we first glimpsed each other across the sparkling ballroom, me in my simple domestic dress and him shining like a knight. I said he must have thought me a rag picker, sitting on the rocks barefoot. He laughed and said I was the most beautiful rag picker he'd ever seen and he'd been searching for me the whole night, trying to escape a debutant, one Miss Courtney Morgan, who'd been chasing him down. Didn't I know I saved his life that night? With his arm around me and my head on his shoulder we watched the fireworks. It is always a thrill. The ships in the ocean all aglow, the lanterns from the Japanese Garden swaying in the soft breeze, the roar and zing of the fireworks as they ascend to heaven. He took my hand and we strolled along towards the garden and sat on a bench. He bent toward me and gently kissed my eyes, my nose, my lips, then holding my hands knelt before me. I will remember his words forever.

"Agnes, more than anything I wanted you to be here with me tonight to remember the magic of our first meeting, I have loved you from the moment I saw you, a brilliant light who entered my heart and never dimmed. Will you do me the honor of becoming my wife?" A soft peace came over me, for the earth had stopped spinning on its axis, and I was finally home. I touched my hand to his cheek and said I too loved him. Then he placed a pearl ring on my finger, a pearl from Japan he always knew would be mine. He swept me into his arms and kissed me so deeply I thought I might faint. I entwined myself around his tall strength and said, "Kiss me again, my one true love." And he did.

July 15, 1911

I've been the belle of the ball, and though it takes some getting used to, I'm liking it for sure. The day after our engagement, Patsy and Eugene, Christian's parents, called us at the yacht club and were very happy for us. Barbara and Wesley had a lovely luncheon for us at the Cliff House with Norah and Tom and the Commander and Mrs. Commander. Oh, that Loretta! She simpered around with a tight little smile, devastated her favorite nephew was marrying a commoner.

When all the excitement of our engagement finally settled down, Barbara and Wesley asked us to have a quiet picnic lunch with them at Easton's Beach. Christian thought something was up as we had both noticed they seemed a bit distracted during the weekend. We had just settled at a picnic table when they both reached across it, took our hands and said, "We need your help to elope." We just stared at them with surprise, but then it all became clear. Barbara said Loretta was acting like she was the virgin bride

(I blushed at that) and Barbara did not want an extravaganza, but she just carries on despite her protests.

"We just want to begin our lives together," Barbara said. "I am a twenty-seven-year-old divorced woman and it is way past the time I get out of mother's clutches." Luckily Christian had ten days before he had to report for duty, so the plan was hatched.

We took the Fall River Line back to New York together, Wesley to return to work and Barbara made up a story that she was to meet with Thomas Hunter. Wesley had arranged for a judge friend of his to marry them in his chambers at the New York County Courthouse. When the ship docked in New York a photographer from the New York Gazette took our picture and asked our names. Wesley said Mr. and Mrs. Wesley Myers. We laughed ourselves silly at the uproar that will cause.

Three days later we were witnesses at their wedding. Barbara was a dream in pale blue silk and carried a bouget of baby's breath and roses. I wore my soft pink frock from the night Christian proposed. After the ceremony, we went to the Palm Court at the Plaza for a celebration lunch. I thought of the time Barbara brought me there with Loretta and what an uncomfortable soul I was amidst the glamor. Now I just marched right in with Christian on my arm and settled nicely in a velvet chair beneath a stately palm.

New York City
July 20, 1911
It's been a week of wonder and gaiety and more surprises. It seemed the whole of Maiden Lane was waiting on our arrival at the inn. I have to say we were hugged nearly to the death. John popped open

the Jamison's and offered an Irish toast. Then Maureen asked if we had set a date. Well, of course we hadn't we said, we were too busy getting Barbara and Wesley married. Oh, what a story to be told and the glee with which it was received.

As the afternoon waned and the excitement dwindled Christian and I strolled to the river. I could tell he had a bit of something in his handsome head. "You know, my darling, Maureen is right. We should set a date." Set a date! I was just getting used to having his ring on my finger, but before I could squeak a word out he went on. "I love you so much, and when I return from my tour in December we can marry and begin our life together wherever I am posted. I don't think I can bear to live without you."

I stopped breathing for a moment as the reality of this new life awaiting gripped me in wonder. "A moment," I said and walked to the railing at the edge of the river filling my lungs with the salt scented air. When I turned back he was pacing on the promenade and strode to me. "Agnes, my love, have I upset you?" I touched a finger to his lips and said, "December in New York is my favorite time of year."

July 30, 1911
Christiane only had five days in New York before his deployment and we knew we had to meet with a priest to set the date before he left. I thought we could be married at St. Peter's on Barkley Street for that is where I attended mass with the Galvin's. So, we're sitting in the parlor just moonin' away and Christian says his father went to school with Father O'Malley at St. Patrick's and we could be married there. My mind flew back to the girl on the bicycle in awe of the place and Chipper telling me it was everyone's cathedral for all the people of New York.

I said it was a bit overwhelming to think of getting married in a cathedral of all things and he said I was as lovely and worthy as light that shines through its great rose window. Me, a bride at the great St. Patrick's. I know I'm not in Galway anymore!

August 1, 1911
We met with Father O'Malley, a tall and robust figure with a warm smile and both wisdom and humor in his green eyes. He put us at ease, chatting about his days in school with Captain Farrell, and how they both went to sea. And then he asked us about our commitment to each other and the gravity of the Holy Sacrament of Matrimony. Christian said he knew I was his one true love the night we met, and how he boldly wrote and asked to court me. I said I was overcome by the emotion I felt at our first encounter and could barely believe his attentions. Then Father O'Malley said we were steadfast in the adversity of long separations, an inspiration to the power of love and he would be honored to marry us.

"Come now," he said, "let's look at Our Lady Chapel." We entered from a side door into a space behind the sanctuary. We dipped our hands into the holy water font, genuflected and crossed ourselves to be worthy of such an exquisite place of worship. The stained-glass windows behind the statue of Mary flickered like flames in the afternoon sun and quiet worshipers lighted candles and bent their heads in prayer, for Mary is a powerful force. I felt her. I felt her love and guidance and we knelt before her in thanks. Father O'Malley gently touched our shoulders and said, "You will have a beautiful wedding."

August 3, 1911

I asked Maureen to be my matron of honor, and Barbara and Christian's sister, Lucy, to be bridesmaids. Now I'm caught in the whirlwind of Maureen and Barbara planning my wedding. You'd think I was the bloody Queen of England for all the fuss as the two of them put their shining heads together to get me down the aisle. They were something to behold.

I hurried off to work and they poured over catalogs like two magpies in a nest, zipping tea and munching on scones, a baby on each lap. They didn't even miss me.

Mum sent me some of her Irish Sweepstakes money for my gown for she said it was only right, and we set off to find a pattern and material. Now I didn't want some full up concoction with tulle and lace and a train I'd be trippin' over. They agreed and said I had a classic beauty and a fine figure I should accentuate. That's what they said, "accentuate." Praise be Jesus.

We chose a pattern for a simple yet elegant empire style gown with a softly gathered neckline and a bit of a puff sleeve that narrowed to the wrist. Then Chipper's mom, who was the seamstress, took us to a fabric store. It was there I found a heavy ivory satin I thought would suit me. The girls thought it was a perfect choice instead of pure white against my black hair and dark eyes.

Maureen said she would be honored if I wore her veil, simple and sweet held by a band of pearls.

Then they set about choosing their attendants gowns. I did say I wanted a touch of green somewhere to honor me Irish roots, and we decided on short velvet caplets in a deep emerald over cream crepe. Here we come!

My Wedding Day

Christian and I were married at Our Lady Chapel in St. Patrick's Cathedral on December 15th. The bright December sun sent prisms of blue light through the stained-glass windows and I felt the glow from within as John walked me down the aisle. Christian's mother, Patsy, was smiling and lovely in pale pink, and Aunt Loretta was doing her best not to grimace. Norah and Tom made the journey here for they adore Christian. The Commander and the Captain stood at attention in their dress blues, each with a sword at his side. Christian's brother stood beside him as best man. Maureen, Barbara and Lucy joined them at the altar.

I kept my gaze on Christian who seemed a prince so tall and handsome in his uniform. As his brilliant blue eyes focused on mine the joy of us enveloped me. When I passed Chipper, Eileen and Francis and my friends from school my heart was full, yet a part of it held a deep sadness that my Mum and Pa and loved ones in Ireland could not bear witness.

Praise the Lord, I made it down the aisle without tripping on my gown, but John had a good hold on me. When I reached the altar, Christian stepped down, took my hand and we knelt before Father O'Malley. He leaned toward us, smiled and said we were a beautiful couple, and then with a sparkle in his eyes said, "Now, are you ready?" Then he began. "Agnes and Christian, you are about to enter into the Holy Sacrament of Matrimony." And so, we were wed.

As we recessed the chapel we were escorted to the great bronze doors and there on the steps of the cathedral stood six officers of the great United States Navy stood at full attention. One announced, "Arch sabers!" and we ducked beneath them to the delight of the spectators who hooted and hollered.

After the ceremony, Maureen and John hosted a repast at the inn, warmed by the fireplace, plentiful spirits, and heaping tables of food. Even Loretta seemed to relax, but it is hard to resist the charms of such generous and loving people. Christian had his father's car so we drove to a secluded inn on the Hudson and let our love be our guide.

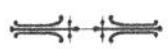

January 1, 1912
Today is New Year's Day and I lit a candle at Mass for all the gifts God has bestowed on this once weary traveler. I walked out to South Ferry breathin' in the crisp January air and thought of the ragged bundle who stepped off the boat nearly six years past. It was quiet at the docks but I bought some hot chestnuts from a red-faced vendor.

As I strolled along eating my chestnuts I thought of finding John Galvin in the crowd, of my journey to Newport, meeting Norah and Barbara, and how my service to her changed my life. It is true that an act of kindness has ripples one cannot see until they reach the shore.

To think of it. I took off my gloves and held my left hand up to the sun, admiring my wedding ring, I know the blessings bestowed on our union will keep us anchored wherever the winds of the sea lead us. I am, after all, a Navy wife. Christian, who knows my heart deeply, said I can teach or counsel anywhere. That is a source of comfort for me as I leave the embrace of my home at Hunter.

Fey always said I was the brave one, but I'm thinking that I was led by some higher force and kept moving toward a light I could not yet see, quaking in my boots and blessing myself all along the way.

This wonderful Christmas season our joy was shared with all those we hold dear, and we wandered through the city enjoying the festive sights and sounds. He tucked my arm in his and we strolled along Fifth Avenue as snowflakes began to fall. Then he bent and kissed a snowflake off my nose and I embraced my unexpected life.

EPILOGUE

March 1, 1912

Dear Sis,

So, you got yerself married to that sailor boy! Oh, I would have loved to see my high falutin' sister walkin' down that aisle of St. Patrick's full of Irish gumption. I'd be sayin' we're part of this new grand century, movin' as fast as those fancy cars and underground trains, and maybe even this amazin' ship I've been buildin' with my boys.

Can you believe it? I'll be workin' me way across the great Atlantic for they'll be needin' my engineering skills. We'll be slippin' into the channel and headin' for Southampton and Queensland to take on passengers and crew and then on to New York City.

Now, sis, you'll be needin' to sit down for this next bit of news. I got it in me fine Irish head that Ma and Pa could make the journey with me. Then Fey was tellin' us she and James were planning on a trip one day to see some fancy doctor in New York. It took a bit of doin' to get Pa and his pipe away from the hearth, so set in his ways he is. Ma was all a flutter at first, sayin' she's only been as far as Dublin in her whole life, but Fey said she'd be by her side all the way. Now Ma is flaunting her good fortune around Ballygar and Mrs. O'Hara's envy is greener than the sod. Now the deal is done, and they'll all be boardin' in Queensland. It will be the grandest of adventures headin' across the ocean in the finest and fastest ship ever built, the unsinkable Titanic.

Your best brother,
Charlie

ABOUT THE AUTHOR

Rosaleen Rooney Myers is the author of "Uncle Raymond's Garden," a memoir about her mother's family in Newport, R.I., and co-author of "Three Brown Eyed Girls," memoir and poetry about the lives of three women. Her "The Secrets of Beacon Hill," is a young adult mystery.

Rosaleen was born in New York City, and as a young woman worked at ABC News where she met her husband, settled in New Jersey and raised two children. When she was in her forties she attended Ramapo College of New Jersey and received a B.A. in Communication Arts, then began a new career as the Development Director.

She and her husband, Jerry, are retired and live in the seaside town of Ocean Grove, NJ, a National Historic District. She served on the board of the Historical Society of Ocean Grove and is the Vice President of the Shore Action League, a philanthropic organization. She is a member of the Jersey Shore Writers at the Jersey Shore Arts Center.

Rosaleen can be reached at jerro@optonline.net or rosaleenmyers@me.com.

BIBLIOGRAPHY

The Memoirs of Admiral H. Kent Hewitt
Edited by Evelyn M. Cherpak
Naval War College Press
Newport, RI
2004

The Archives of the Alumni Association of Hunter College
1872-2008

Made in the USA
Columbia, SC
15 February 2018